Marshall Mather

John Ruskin

His Life and Teaching - Vol. 1

Marshall Mather

John Ruskin
His Life and Teaching - Vol. 1

ISBN/EAN: 9783337241957

Printed in Europe, USA, Canada, Australia, Japan

Cover: Foto ©Raphael Reischuk / pixelio.de

More available books at **www.hansebooks.com**

JOHN RUSKIN:

HIS LIFE AND TEACHING.

BY

J. MARSHALL MATHER.

FOURTH EDITION.

LONDON AND NEW YORK:
FREDERICK WARNE AND CO.
1892.

PREFACE TO THIRD EDITION.

As announced in prefaces of earlier editions, this little book lays no claim to be either a criticism or defence. It is simply an outline of Ruskin's life and teaching, intended for those who are purposing a careful and detailed study of his works.

In the preparation of this new edition I have availed myself of advice tendered by those who criticised the book in its earlier and cruder forms. While the bulk of the book remains the same, the first chapter has been re-written, and enlarged with facts gathered from " Præterita."

The rank which Ruskin as a teacher is likely to hold in coming years forms the subject of an additional chapter.

J. M. M.

RAWTENSTALL,
    October, 1890.

CONTENTS.

CHAPTER VII.

CHAPTER VIII.

CHAPTER IX.

CHAPTER X.

JOHN RUSKIN.

CHAPTER I.

PARENTAGE, YOUTH, MANHOOD.

ANCESTRY, disposition, and education are the three cardinal points determining the course and the consequence of human existence. Ancestry ranks first, for intellectual and moral greatness are hereditary; and though all great sons may not have had great fathers, the germ of their greatness lies somewhere in their families' past. In the quantity and quality of this inherited greatness, or, in other words, in disposition, the possibilities and attainments of the man are foreshadowed, for no one can rise above himself, nor become truly great in any other orbit save the one fixed for him at birth, and correspondent to his bent and natural powers. As for education, it is an instrument only, and limited by the potentiality of the material upon which it is brought to bear. It matters little how comprehensive and thorough it may be as a system ; apart from the great laws of selection and development it remains powerless as a force in the improvement of the race. Thus, man is a product of the

past as well as a factor in the future—a meeting-point as
well as a starting-point, all that radiates from him being con-
trolled by that converging in him.   Hence, he who would
faithfully estimate a man's life and labours must not only
know what the man has himself done, but what others have
done for him and in him, for, apart from the interpretative
light of antecedents, the simplest and most uneventful life is
enigmatical and unknown.

Fortunately, John Ruskin has left on record in the pages
of "Fors Clavigera" and "Præterita" a detailed summary
of those forces that went to form his character, and that lie
at the source of his achievements.   As this summary is carefully noted and followed, it is clearly seen that the child's
destiny was fixed for him long before his birth, and that
from his earliest years the boy became the father of the man.
His father's youthful energies were roused by certain monetary misfortunes that overtook the family in Scotland,
driving him at an early age from Perth to London, where
he drudged for nine years in a merchant's office, and never
sought a holiday until he had been successful in paying off
the old debts, and vindicating the reputation of his father's
name.

Although engaged in commercial pursuits, the father of
John Ruskin was no mere city drudge.   He was a man of
considerable culture, and familiar with literature and art.
His favourite authors were the English classics, and much
of his spare time was spent in pen-and-ink sketching, as
well as in studying the productions of the old masters.
The earlier part of the day he devoted to business ; but
after noon his steps were turned homewards, and his mind

given to his favourite studies. The chief of his few faults was a dislike of being excelled, and he never forgave those who in his own sphere approached him in equality. Next to trustworthiness, incapacity was the chief feature he sought in the subordinates he employed. This fault doubled his labours and increased his anxiety; nevertheless, it gratified his pardonable pride. Many men of note, amongst whom were artists and scholars, gathered round his table; nor were the city magnates infrequent visitors. Concerning these latter, his son says: "Very early in my boy's life, I began much to dislike these commercial feasts, and to form, by carefully attending to their dialogue, when it chanced to turn on any other subject than wine, an extremely low estimate of the commercial mind as such—estimate which I have never had the slightest reason to alter." Apart from this criticism, his estimate of his father, and of his father's friends, was high; for in another passage he, in speaking of some of them, says: "They were flawless types of the London citizen of olden days—incorruptible, proud with sacred and humble pride, happy in their function and position, putting daily their total energy into the detail of their business duties, and finding daily a refined and perfect pleasure in the hearth-side poetry of domestic life . . . romantic as girls . . . inflexible as soldier recruits on any matter of probity and honour, in business and out of it . . . hating Radical newspapers, and devoted to the House of Lords; my father only, it seemed to me, slightly failing in his loyalty to the Worshipful the Mayor and Corporation of London."

John Ruskin's maternal grandfather was a seafaring man,

making frequent, and at times long, voyages from Yarmouth. He combined the fondness of a father with the sternness of a disciplinarian, and was relentless in punishment if his commands were disobeyed. On one occasion, when a child, the mother of John Ruskin told her seafaring parent a lie, consequent upon which he sent his servant for a bundle of new broom-twigs wherewith to whip her. The impression produced by this correction may be best given in her own words : "They did not hurt me so much as *one* would have done, but I *thought* a good deal of it." He died while his children were young, and this said daughter, after being educated with her sisters at a school in Croydon, was sent into Scotland to take charge of the house of her reckless old uncle, the father of the before-named industrious London clerk. Here she moved in a higher sphere of society, " a tall, handsome, finely-made girl, with a beautiful mild firmness of expression ; a faultless and accomplished housekeeper, and a natural, essential, unassailable, yet inoffensive prude." "Ah, Miss Margaret," said an old Scotch servant to her one day, "ah, Miss Margaret, ye are just like Martha, carefu' and troubled about mony things."

Margaret, now twenty years of age, not only fulfilled the office of a careful and skilled housekeeper, but became, in part, the governess and the confidante of her " dark-eyed, brilliantly active and sensitive " cousin, who was four years her junior, assisting him, and sympathizing with him in his domestic and business sorrows. This relation was long continued without a thought on either side of marriage. When, however, it was determined he should commence his business career in London, he asked her if her attachment was such as to warrant the promise of wedlock, and if her patience could bide the time demanded on his part to earn for her an independency. To both these she assented, and then followed an engagement of nine years, during which Margaret gave proof of her affection in fitting herself by hard study for companionship with the man whom she counted so greatly her superior; and John showed his honourable love by unremitting attention to his work. Finally, they were married in Perth one evening after supper, forming what proved to be a most fitting union, and commencing a long life of domestic calm, culture, and happiness.

John Ruskin was their only child, and born in London on February 8, 1819. As a boy he was closely observant, his recollections of life dating from his fourth year. Of these recollections we have some charming fragments in the pages of "Fors Clavigera." They give us glimpses of a little boy reverently watching his father at work on sketches in indian-ink; of a loving mother; of a fond aunt with Evangelical tendencies, enforcing cold mutton dinners on Sunday because it was the day of rest; of pleasant holidays at Croydon spent in romps upon the Duppas Hill, or the heather at Addington; with strange adventures in his uncle's bakehouse, and hours of childish musing round "the spring of crystal water at the back door." When he was three years and a half old he stood for his portrait, and being asked by the artist, Northcote, what he would like for the background of the painting, replied, "Blue hills." At the age of five he was a voracious reader, sending to the circulating library for his favourite books.

The home rule of his mother was well-nigh puritanic in its severity; his toys were few, and his sources of amusement limited. He says: "For toys I had a bunch of keys to play with, as long as I was capable of pleasure in what glittered and jingled; as I grew older I had a cart and a ball; and when I was five or six years old, two boxes of well-cut wooden bricks. With these modest but, I still think, entirely sufficient possessions, and being always summarily whipped if I cried, did not do as I was bid, or tumbled on the stairs, I soon attained serene and secure methods of life and motion, and could pass my days contentedly in tracing the squares and comparing the colours of my carpet; examining the knots in the wood of the floor, or counting the bricks in the opposite houses; with rapturous intervals of excitement during the filling of the water-cart, through its leathern pipe, from the dripping iron post at the pavement edge; or the still more admirable proceedings of the turn-cock, when he turned and turned until a fountain sprang up in the middle of the street. But the carpet, and what patterns I could find in bed-covers, dresses, or wall-papers to be examined, were my chief resources."

In the further development of John Ruskin's character we may trace three great formative influences—the influence of home surroundings and parents, the influence of literature, and the influence of nature and art.

More beautiful or healthier domestic environment cannot be imagined than that enjoyed by him in the days of his Herne Hill boyhood. The little estate was situated upon the crown of the hill, and four miles distant from the heart of city life. Hidden in seclusion, and free from innovation, its upper windows on either side commanded views of the Norwood hills, and the winter sunrise over them and the Valley of the Thames. The house was fronted by a garden of old evergreens and well-grown lilacs and laburnums, and a large plot of beneficent ground ran out from the rear, rich in fruit-trees and gay with flowers. In this orchard splendour of colour abounded; "fresh green, soft amber, and rough-bristled crimson bending the spinous branches, and clustered pearl and pendent ruby joyfully discoverable under the large leaves that looked like vine." Here the boy wandered and wondered, perplexing his mind as to how it was that while one tree only was forbidden in Eden, all the trees in this garden were placed under ban, and lamenting that the companionable beasts once surrounding his Adamic forefather were not found at his side. "Otherwise," he says, "the little domain answered every purpose of Paradise to me; and the climate, in that cycle of years, allowed me to pass most of my life in it."

Within the home there was a reign of perfect order, un-broken peace, and disciplined joy. His father and mother lived with strict economy, never spending more than half their yearly income, keeping only female servants, using only tallow candles in plated candlesticks, and content with their leasehold territory of front and back garden. "I never heard," says Ruskin, "my father's or mother's voice once raised in any question with each other; nor saw an angry, or even slightly hurt or offended, glance in the eyes of either. I never heard a servant scolded, nor even suddenly, passion-ately, or in any severe manner blamed. I never saw a moment's trouble or disorder in any household matter; nor

anything whatever either done in a hurry, or undone in due
time."

Early every morning the boy John was admitted into his
father's dressing-room, where he was particularly fond of
watching him shave. Over the dressing-table hung a water-
colour sketch made by the father's own hand when a boy at
the High School of Edinburgh, and when the shaving was
over, of which the son was a "motionless witness," the
parent called his attention to the picture, and wove out of
his fancies stories supposed to be associated with it. In the
afternoon, after the father's return from business, and after
the half-past four dinner, the child was placed in a little
recess in the drawing-room, a cup of milk and slice of bread-
and-butter before him on a small table. Here, like "an
idol in a niche," he sat while his mother knitted, and his
father read aloud from the Waverley novels, or some other
famous English classic. In the summer-time these evening
gatherings were in the garden, beneath the trees.

No wonder Ruskin speaks fondly of "the salutary pleasures
of Herne Hill," and traces to its sacred environment his
spiritual possessions of peace, obedience, and faith. He
also claims as outcome of this early training the intellectual
power of fixed attention, and a sensuous perfection of palate
and all other senses. Set off, however, against these
pleasures and beneficial fruits of childhood were equally
dominant calamities, resultant from the fact that he had
nothing to love, nothing to endure, and was taught no precision nor etiquette of manners. His words are: "My
parents were, in a sort, visible powers of nature to me, no
more loved than the sun and the moon; only I should have

been annoyed and puzzled if either of them had gone out ;
still less did I love God ; not that I had any quarrel with
Him, or fear of Him ; but simply found what people told
me was His service, disagreeable ; and what people told me
was His book, not entertaining. . . . Danger and pain of
any kind I knew not ; my strength was never exercised, my
patience never tried, and my courage never fortified. . . .
My present verdict, therefore, on the general tenor of my
education at this time must be, that it was at once too
formal and too luxurious ; leaving my character, at the most
important moment for its construction, cramped indeed, but
not disciplined ; and only by protection innocent, instead of
by practice virtuous."

The books chosen for him by his mother, and which he
regularly read aloud in her presence, were Pope's translation
of Homer, and the novels of Sir Walter Scott ; these were
for week-day instruction : for the Sabbath were reserved
" Robinson Crusoe " and " Pilgrim's Progress." In addition
to these he daily read aloud, and committed to memory,
portions of the Bible.   He owes much to this instruction in
the Word of God, received at his mother's knee, and never
wearies of referring to it with expressions of deepest gratitude.
He says : " My mother forced me by steady, patient, daily
toil, to learn long chapters of the Bible by heart, as well as
to read it every syllable through, aloud, hard names and all,
from Genesis to the Apocalypse, about once every year ; and
to that discipline—patient, accurate, and resolute—I owe,
not only a knowledge of the book I find occasionally serviceable, but much of my general power of taking pains, and
the best part of my taste in literature.   From Walter Scott

I might easily, as I grew older, have fallen to other people's
novels, and Pope might have led me to take Johnson's English, or Gibbon's, as types of language, but once knowing the
xxxii. of Deuteronomy, cxix. Psalm, xiii. of 1st Corinthians,
the Sermon on the Mount, and most of the Apocalypse,
every syllable by heart, and having always a way of thinking
with myself what words meant, it was not possible for me,
even in the foolishest time of youth, to write entirely superficial or formal English, and the affectation of trying to write
like Hooker or George Herbert was the most innocent I
could have fallen into."

Or again, what can be more touching than the following
reference to the same subject in another part of his writings?
—"I opened my oldest Bible just now . . . yellow, now,
with age, and flexible, but not unclean, with much use,
except that the lower corners of the pages at the viii. ch. of
1st Book of Kings and the xxxii. ch. of Deuteronomy are
worn somewhat thin and dark, the learning of these two
chapters having caused me much pains. My mother's list
of chapters with which, learned every syllable accurately, she
established my soul in life, has just fallen out of it, as
follows : ' Exodus xv. and xx. ; II. Samuel i. ch., from 17 v.
to end ; I. Kings viii. ; Psalms xxiii., xxxii., xc., xci., ciii.,
cxii., cxix., cxxxix; Proverbs ii., iii., viii., xii. ; Isaiah lviii. ;
Matthew v., vi., vii. ; Acts xxvi. : I. Corinthians xiii., xv. ;
James iv. ; Revelation v., vi.'   And truly, though I have
picked up the elements of a little further knowledge . . .
in mathematics, meteorology, and the like, in after-life, and
owe not a little to the teaching of many people, this maternal
installation of my mind in that property of chapters, I count

very confidently the most precious, and, on the whole, the
one essential part of all my education. For the chapters
became, indeed, strictly conclusive and protective to me in
all modes of thought, and the body of divinity they contain,
acceptable through all fear or doubt : nor through any
fear or doubt or fault have I ever lost my loyalty to them,
nor betrayed the first command in the one I was made to
repeat oftenest, ' Let not mercy and truth forsake thee.' "

These are noble words ; and such testimony, from one of
the foremost men in thought and literature, is indeed cheer-
ing to those who still retain reverence for the "written
Word." The best defenders of the Bible are men who, like
John Ruskin, have proved its value from life-long embodiment of its principles ; and compared with their defence,
the special pleadings of doctrinaires and apologists go for
little. That is a baseless faith which relies solely upon
external pleas. Those who know the Bible best believe
most in its authority. To such, and to such alone, the Book
becomes what it became to John Ruskin—"conclusive and
protective " ; and when once its conclusiveness and protec-
tiveness are realized, it matters little who attacks it, inasmuch
as it has given irrefragable proof that its commandments
are exceeding broad, and that in the keeping of them there
is life.

From earliest years Ruskin was susceptible to the influences of nature, his child-eye fastening with delight and
wonder on all inanimate things. The sky above, the pebbles
beneath, the flowers and foliage around—these from infancy
led him into regions of romance and wonderland, while the
hills rebuked his weaknesses and purified his heart. The

stony bed of the crystal Wandle at Croydon, and the shallow
pools of the pausing Tay at Perth, left lasting impressions
upon his opening mind ; and a stay at Matlock, when he
was eleven years of age, gave a start and shape to his future
mineralogical studies. As a boy, his heart leapt within him
as he looked upon the Alps, "beautiful in their snow and
humanity," and it was in an evening walk from the garden-
terrace of Schaffhausen that his destiny was fixed in all that
was to be sacred and useful. His parents devoted much of
the summer season to travel, at home and abroad. This
arrangement was greatly facilitated in that his father, though
senior partner, was the provincial and Continental agent for
the large firm of vintners known as Ruskin, Telford, and
Domecq. In those days the rush and competition of life
were not such as to call for the overtaxing commercial habits
common in our own time. In a postchaise, with a seat
specially fitted up for the boy John, and from which he had
good view of all surrounding objects, the wine-merchant of
the olden type slowly drove to receive his orders and settle
his accounts. Whenever some lovely landscape opened out
before him he would stop to take full measure of the scene,
and call the child's attention to its beauties. Now and
again, alighting from the chaise, they would together stroll
along some bypath or hedgerow, looking into the beauty of
a flower, or gazing in rapture at some lovely nook where
Nature had lavished her richest gifts of fern and foliage.
Thus, passing through many of the choicest English counties,
as well as visiting the grandest Continental scenery, the
boy's soul expanded as he beheld with admiration and awe
the handiwork of God. His own words are as follows :

"I possess the gift of taking pleasure in landscape in a greater degree than most men. . . . The first thing I remember as an event in life, was being taken by my nurse to the brow of 'Friar's Crag,' on Derwentwater. The intense joy, mingled with awe, that I had in looking through the mossy roots over the crag into the dark lake, has associated itself more or less with all twining roots of trees ever since. Two other things I remember, as, in a sort, beginnings of life—crossing Shap-fells (being let out of the chaise to run up the hill), and going through Glen Farg, near Kinross, on a winter's morning when the rocks were hung with icicles; these being culminating points in an early life of more travelling than is usually indulged in to a child. In such journeyings, whenever they brought me near hills, and in all mountain ground and scenery, I had a pleasure, as early as I can remember, and continuing until I was eighteen or twenty, infinitely greater than any which has been since possible to me in anything, comparable for intensity only to the joy of a lover, in being near a noble and kind mistress, but no more explicable or definable than love itself."

As with nature, so with art: from a boy he intuitively responded to its suggestions and entered into its revelations. In all this he found a wise teacher and sympathetic companion in his father, whose passionate and discriminating taste for pictures was forming for him a friendship with many of the first artists of his day. Whenever father and son in their travels came near any gentleman's house famed for its collection of pictures, they would delay the journey in order to devote an hour or two to their inspection. In

speaking of his father's tastes, he says : "My father had a
quite infallible natural judgment in painting, and though it
had never been cultivated, so as to enable him to understand the Italian schools, his sense of the power of the
northern masters was as true and passionate as that of the
most accomplished artist.   He never, when I was old enough
to care for what he himself delighted in, allowed me to look
at a bad picture."

Such were the surroundings and impressions of Ruskin
during the first decade of his life.   Reverent in disposition,
his father and mother, by their integrity and firmness, confirmed him in that great essential apart from which no true
character is formed.   Sensitive to all that was beautiful in
thought, in scenery, and in expression, it was his fortune
from his earliest years to be directed to the healthy in literature, the sublime in nature, and the perfect in art.   Analytic
in mind, he was permitted, without hindrance and without
hurry, to look at and to look into the objects around him ;
nor was he corrected when he questioned for information,
or ventured his verdict upon the themes that from the first
troubled his childish brain.   Summing up his temperament
and tendencies throughout these years, he says : "I had in
my little clay pitcher vialsful, as it were, of Wordsworth's
reverence, Shelley's sensitiveness, Turner's accuracy, all in
one.   A snowdrop was to me, as to Wordsworth, part of the
Sermon on the Mount ; but I never should have written
sonnets to the celandine, because it is of a coarse yellow,
and imperfect in form.   With Shelley, I loved blue sky and
blue eyes, but never in the least confused the heavens with
my own poor little Psychidion.   And the reverence and the

passion were alike kept in their places by the constructive
Turnerian element; and I did not weary myself in wishing
that a daisy could see the beauty of its shadow, but in trying
to draw the shadow rightly myself."

As early as 1834, when Ruskin was but fifteen years of
age, he mapped out and pursued the following fourfold
course of work : expression of genuine sentiment in rhyme ;
engraving ; study of architecture ; and the gratification of
early geological instinct.   In his self-criticism of the advance
he made in this "quadrilateral plan," he tells of the liking
he had for staring at the sea or scampering over the moor,
and then of trying to make melodious noise about them,
like the waves or the peewits.   In after-years, when survey-
ing with trained eye his early attempts at engraving, his
remark is : "I have never seen drawing by a youth so
entirely industrious in delicate line ; and there was really
the making of a fine landscape, or figure outline, engraver
in me."   With all Ruskin's love for architecture, and despite
the interpretative light he has thrown upon that glorious
science, he affirms that he was always without power of
design ; while the instinct for mineralogy led him at the age
of fifteen to select Saussure's "Voyages dans les Alps" as a
birthday gift, and pursue with unabated zest his progressive
study in the mountain regions of the Alps.

Apart from a few lessons in Greek taken from Dr.
Andrews, the whole of Ruskin's early tuition was received
at the feet of his mother. The influence of this noble woman
cannot be over-estimated—indeed, what he owes to her is
beyond computation.   She was a rigid disciplinarian, yet
free from the spirit of the martinet ; for while always making

her boy master his tasks, she never set him more than it was within his power to master. She carefully allotted his hours of work, discriminately selected his subjects for study, and patiently enforced the scheme planned for his early and home tuition—on one occasion holding her self-willed pupil for three weeks at the couplet

> "Shall any following spring revive
> The ashes of the urn?"

before she succeeded in getting him to rightly accent the word "of": and, as Ruskin says, if it had taken her three years instead of three weeks, she would have held out, having once undertaken to do it. Strange to say, he did not learn to read by syllables. He would get an entire sentence off by heart, and then point to every word as he repeated it, learning whole words at a time.

From the tuition of his mother he passed into the school-room of the Rev. Thomas Dale. It was upon his entrance into this school that he met with the first of the world's rebuffs; and so touchingly has he described it, that it would be foolish to recount it in other than his own words:

"On the first day when I went to take my seat in Mr. Dale's schoolroom, I carried my old grammar to him, in a modest pride, expecting some encouragement and honour for the accuracy with which I could repeat, on demand, some hundred and sixty printed pages of it. But Mr. Dale threw it back to me with a fierce bang upon his desk, saying (with accent and look of seven-times-heated scorn), 'That's a SCOTCH thing!' Now, my father being Scotch, and an Edinburgh High School boy, and my mother having laboured in that book with me since I could read, and all my happiest holiday time having been spent on the North Inch of Perth, these four words, with the action accompanying them, contained so much insult, pain, and loosening of my respect for my parents, love of my father's country, and honour for its worthies, as it was possible to compress into four syllables, and an ill mannered gesture. . . . To make a boy despise his mother's care, is the straightest way also to make him despise his Redeemer's voice ; and to make him scorn his father and his father's house, the straightest way to make him despise his God."

From this school he went to Christ Church, Oxford, and found himself transferred to the centre of a great life. Those were the times of " feast of reason and flow of soul " ; and the set with whom John Ruskin associated gave unmistakable and literal adhesion to this order of the day. It was then customary to feast and fuddle at the college suppers until many of the undergraduates were carried out in a state of helpless intoxication. Describing one such, he says : " Thirty years ago, I, a most inexperienced freshman, went to my first college supper. At the head of the table sat a nobleman of high promise and of admirable powers, since dead of palsy. There, also, we had in the midst of us, not buckets, indeed, but bowls as large as buckets ; there, also, we helped ourselves with ladles. There (for this beginning of college life was compulsory) I, choosing ladlefuls of punch instead of claret, because I was then able, unperceived, to pour them into my waistcoat instead of down my throat, stood it out to the end, and helped to carry four of my fellow-students, one of them the son of the head of a college, head foremost, downstairs and home."

2

Ruskin, however, in his Oxford career, was proof against temptation of this order. Excess of all kinds disgusted him ; nor had the gambling spirit any hold upon him. Up to his entering Oxford he had never touched a card ; and as for dice, he tells us he looked upon them as people now look upon dynamite. Nor was there danger of his running in debt, for, as he jocularly hints, " No Turners were to be had in Oxford, and I cared for nothing else in the world of material possession." His conceit, upon his own confession, was armour-proof against all ridicule, the only doubt he had concerning himself being his power to fall in with the three years' work. His desire, however, to do credit to his parents begot within him a strong resolution to succeed, which he eventually fulfilled. Throughout the three years of his Oxford residence, his mother lodged in the High Street, to be near him, and to take care of him, his father coming down from Herne Hill at the end of each week, the three attending Sunday by Sunday the morning service at St. Peter's. Ruskin leaves it on record that throughout the whole of his college career no one ever said a word in depreciation of this pardonable fondness on the part of his parents, or of his compliance with their old-fashioned life.

One of his co-temporaries at Oxford was the late Frederick William Robertson, of Brighton—a man who attained as great distinction in the realm of theology as Ruskin in the realm of art criticism. While fellow-students they crossed swords in a memorable debate, the particulars of which are given as follows in Stopford Brooke's " Life and Letters of Robertson " : " On one of the occasions on which I paid

Robertson a short visit at Oxford, I went with him to the Union. He was to speak that evening. The subject of debate was the moral tendency, or otherwise, of the theatre. Robertson opened the discussion. I sat next to him, and he was somewhat nervous, it being about the second time that he had spoken. Before he got up to speak, pressing his hand upon my knee, he whispered in my ear, 'Davies, pray for me.' The tenor of his observations was opposed to the idea that theatrical representations could legitimately be made the channel of conveying any really good moral influence or instruction. Robertson was answered by Mr. Ruskin in a very ingenious and somewhat sarcastic speech, which excited much laughter in the room. With considerable circumlocution and innuendo he was describing a certain personage to whose influence he probably thought Robertson had, in his observations, given too much consideration, when Robertson said in my ear, 'Why, the man is describing the devil.'"

While at Oxford Ruskin was successful in competition for the Newdigate Prize Poem. It is entitled "Salsette and Elephanta," and describes the dawn of Christianity in Hindustan. The poem is pervaded by a deeply religious tone, at times almost evangelical; and the metre reminds one of that adopted at times by Pope. It was recited in the Theatre, Oxford, on June 12, 1839, and closes with the following description of the universal spread of Christianity:

> " Yes—he shall fall, though once his throne was set
> Where the high heaven and crested mountains met ;
> Though distant shone with many an azure gem
> The glacier glory of his diadem ;

Though sheets of sulphurous cloud and wreathed storm
Cast veil of terror round his shadowy form.
All, all are vain!   It comes, the hallowed day,
Whose dawn shall rend that robe of fear away ;
Then shall the torturing spells that midnight knew
Far in the cloven dells of Mount Meru,
Then shall the moan of frenzied hymns, that sighed
Down the dark vale where Gunga's waters glide,
Then shall the idol chariots' thunder cease
Before the steps of them that publish peace.
Already are they heard,—how fair, how fleet !
Along the mountains flash their bounding feet !
Disease and death before their presence fly ;
Truth calls, and gladdened India hears the cry,
Deserts the darkened path her fathers trod,
And seeks redemption from the Incarnate God."

From college he passed into the great battle-plain of life,
finding himself at four-and-twenty in the thickest of the fray.
Roused by what he deemed the unfair and cruel strictures
of the press upon the works of Turner, he addressed himself,
not so much to defend that great painter's reputation, as to
uphold the principles of truth and beauty embodied in his
art.   To this end he issued the first volume of " Modern
Painters," in 1843.   The second volume followed after an
interval of two years.   Inasmuch as the history of this great
work, with his other chief productions, will be dealt with in
a succeeding chapter, it is enough to note here that between
the years 1843 and 1860 there appeared, from his pen,
the five volumes of " Modern Painters," the three volumes
of " Stones of Venice," and a volume entitled " The Seven
Lamps of Architecture."   Since 1860, his writings have
covered a wider range of subject, appearing from time to
time in single volume form, each complete in itself.   Of

these the most noted is " Unto this Last," and the most popular "Sesame and Lilies."

John Ruskin has spent many years in Continental travel. The quaint streets of mediæval cities, the façades of Venice, the art galleries of Italy, the Alps of Switzerland, and the Campagnas of the South, have, in turn, received his closest and most appreciative survey. Concerning them all he has written powerfully and pleasingly ; and if any would read of their past histories, and know something of their wealth of loveliness, he can turn to few sources more instructive than those of Ruskin's writings which cover the period of the above travels.

With the exception of a year or two of childhood spent in Brunswick Square, Ruskin resided for upwards of half a century on the Herne Hill and Denmark Hill estates. Here, as elsewhere, he has faithfully followed the teachings laid down in his books. In the " Lamp of Memory," when writing on this subject, he says : " I cannot but think it an evil sign of a people when their houses are built to last for one generation only. There is a sanctity in a good man's house which cannot be renewed in every tenement that rises on its ruins : and I believe that good men would generally feel this ; and that, having spent their lives happily and honourably, they would be grieved, at the close of them, to think that the place of their earthly abode, which had seen, and seemed almost to sympathize in, all their honour, their gladness, or their suffering—that this, with all the record it bare of them, and all of material things that they had loved and ruled over, and set the stamp of themselves upon—was to be swept away, as soon as there was room made for them in the grave; that no respect was to be shown to it, no good to be drawn from it by their children; that though there was a monument in the church, there was no warm monument in the hearth and house to them; that all they had ever treasured was despised, and the places that had sheltered and comforted them were dragged down to the dust. I say that a good man would fear this; and that, far more, a good son, a noble descendant, would fear doing it to his father's house."

John Ruskin has fulfilled the letter and the spirit of this teaching. The house at Herne Hill still stands untouched; and though the encroachments of a so-called modern civilization have destroyed its once rural surrounding, its inner radiancy of sacred memories remains undimmed. Whenever the master journeys to town, he turns to the old roof-tree for shelter, the nursery of his childhood being the room wherein he seeks repose. Speaking of this, his early home, and its once pleasant environments, he says: " In my young days Croxsted Lane was a green bye-road . . . little else than a narrow strip of untilled field, separated by blackberry hedges from the better cared-for meadows on each side of it. There my mother and I used to gather the first buds of the hawthorn; and there, in after-years, I used to walk in the summer shadows, as in a place wilder and sweeter than our garden, to think over any passage I wanted to make better than usual in 'Modern Painters.'"

In 1875 he bought the Brantwood estate for the sum of £1,500, and spent £4,000 more in alterations, additions, and other improvements before it was fit for habitation. The house stands at the foot of a thickly-wooded slope, and

fronts the waters of Coniston.   There is nothing æsthetic
or pretentious either in the structure or its furniture, yet
within its walls is untold wealth.   There hang many of the
Turner drawings, and not a few choice productions from
the brushes of the old masters ; there, too, are to be found
cabinets filled with costly crystals and other precious stones,
with many a relic of the past in shape of missals, black
letter MSS., and mediæval curiosities gathered from the
old cities of Europe ; and there are stored those rows of
" Kings' treasures," the wealth of which is so well known to
their owner, and concerning which he has written with such
attractiveness and profit.   At the angle of one of the rooms,
known as the " turret-chamber," a kind of oriel window
is so constructed that from it the master can not only
see the whole stretch of surrounding country, but also the
rising and the setting of the sun.   Describing dawn from
this outlook, he says : " Morning breaks as I write, along
those Coniston Fells, and the level mists, motionless and
gray beneath the rose of the moorlands, veil the lower
woods, and the sleeping village, and the long lawn by the
lake shore."

From 1870 to 1879 John Ruskin was " Slade Professor
of Art " at the University of Oxford.   Here he soon became
the centre of so great an influence, that he purposely sought
retirement in order to limit the power he was uninten-
tionally wielding over the undergraduates ; and so popular
was he as a lecturer, that, in order to accommodate his
audience, the Sheldonian Theatre was called into use for his
spoken addresses.   It was during his term of professorship
that he led his students, by way of recreation, to manly and

useful toil. "Will none of you," he said, "of your own strength and your leisure do anything for the poor—drain a single cottage, repair a single village bye-way — and you yourselves will be more strong, and your hearts more light, than had your leisure been spent in costly games, or more hurtful amusements." To this noble appeal there was a generous response, and for some time the work was continued with a fair share of success ; but eventually, owing to the laughter of the onlookers and the jeers of the peasantry, the scheme was abandoned.

In politics, John Ruskin calls himself a Conservative, using the term in its original rather than in its accepted sense. He follows principles ; and would select the ablest men for representatives and rulers, independently of all parties. He holds that purity of motive and justness of enactment are the only permanent foundations of government, and concludes that whenever a man, or a body of men, gives proof of inability in legislation, they thereby forfeit all claim to rule, whatever their wealth or rank. The following are his words : " What is to become of the House of Lords ? The answer to such a question depends first upon their being able to answer another question—What is the use of them ? For some time back, I think the theory of the nation has been that they are useful impediments to business, so as to give time for second thoughts. But the nation is getting impatient of impediments to business, and certainly, sooner or later, will think it needless to maintain these expensive obstacles to its humours. And I have not heard, either in public or from themselves, a clear expression of their own conception of their uses. So it seems thus to become needful for all men to tell them, as our one quite-clear-sighted teacher, Carlyle, has been telling us for many a year, that the use of the Lords of a country is to *govern* the country. If they answer that use, the people will rejoice in keeping them; if not, that will become of them which must of all things found to have lost their serviceableness."

John Ruskin, while calling himself a Conservative, is essentially a Radical—nay, he owns to having Communistic tendencies of no uncertain colour. He is impatient of all political tinkering; he hates half-measures, and scorns methods of reformation which begin with the branches and work downward, instead of working from the root upward. He would ask: "Why fine and imprison men for getting drunk, when you create the appetite by the unhealthiness of the toil in which you engage them, and feed the appetite by licensing houses for the sale of adulterated drink? Why play at reducing rents while the peasantry are starving, and you hold back from them their rightful ownership of the land? Why seek to quieten the mass by the bestowment of the franchise, when you care not to bestir yourselves in their social and religious education, and refuse to look at the real root of their dissatisfaction and unrest?" Let the reader bear this in mind, and then he will be better able to understand those torrents of scorn and invective which, from time to time, John Ruskin has brought down upon our political leaders, and which, for the time being, have brought him into such disrepute with the parties thus attacked through their leaders.

Religiously considered, Ruskin belongs to neither party

nor sect. Arraigned before the doctrinaires, he would not
pass muster, for the principles of a universal faith have been
dearer to him than the segments and fragments of eccle-
siastical schools. And yet his whole life, in deeds and in
declaration, has been a steady force making for righteousness. While much of his teaching lies outside the approved
circle of the Church, it still recognises a faith in Divine
Truth and reverence for Divine Mysteries; and he has
never wearied of levelling blows at the pride of Faith which
imagines that the nature of Deity can be defined by its own
convictions, and the pride of Science, which imagines that
the energy of Deity can be explained by its own analysis.
These, however, are the maturer views of his latter years, for
his early training, under his mother, was of the straitest
evangelical type, concerning the character and effects of
which he says : " Her unquestioning faith in the literal truth
of the Bible placed me, as soon as I could conceive and
think, in the presence of an unseen world ; and set my
active analytic power early to work on the questions of conscience, free-will, and responsibility, which are easily determined in days of innocence, but are approached too often
with prejudice, and always with disadvantage, after men
become stupefied by the opinions, or tainted by the sins,
of the outer world." From this faith in the limitations
taught by the leaders of the evangelical school he received
a rude awakening after listening to a sermon in a Waldensian
church, in which the preacher denounced as dishonest and
cut off from hope all those who differed from himself and
his community in declaration of faith and form of worship.
Applying these narrow and hide-bound principles according

to the light of his own logical mind, Ruskin discovered, to
his own horror, that if true they left only a remnant of the
race as participators in salvation, and, as a consequence,
came out of the church having for ever foregone his hitherto
exclusive Protestantism and feeble evangelical faith.   Not
that he ridicules this early religious training, for, upon looking back and comparing his present beliefs with those of the
past, he says : " Whatever I know or feel now of the justice
of God, the nobleness of man, and the beauty of nature, I
knew and felt then, nor less strongly ; but these firm faiths
were confused by the continual discovery, day by day, of
error or limitations in the doctrines I had been taught, and
follies or inconsistencies in their teachers."

In the second volume of " Præterita " he gives us the following estimate of Christianity, and as this is his latest—probably his last—estimate of this faith of faiths, it is worthy of
note: ". . . A firm word concerning Christianity itself.   I find
numbers, even of the most intelligent and amiable people,
not knowing what the word means ; because they are always
asking how much is true, and how much they like, and
never ask, first, what *was* the total meaning of it, whether
they like it or not.   The total meaning was, and is, that the
God who made earth and its creatures took at a certain time
upon the earth the flesh and form of man ; in that flesh
sustained the pain and died the death of the creature He
had made ; rose again after the dead into glorious human
life, and when the date of the human race is ended will
return in visible human form, and render to every man
according to his work.   Christianity is the belief in, and the
love of, God thus manifested.   Anything less than this, the

mere acceptance of the sayings of Christ, or assertion of any less than Divine power in His being, may be, for aught I know, enough for virtue, peace, and safety; but they do not make people Christians, or enable them to understand the heart of the simplest believer in the old doctrine."

We do not care to ask whether this is Ruskin's personal faith or not; indeed, we have scant sympathy with those whose prurient curiosity prompts them to play the part of religious spies, or whose childish anxiety to ally great minds to their own forms of belief inclines them to wrest words unlawfully. The definition, however, as a definition of the old and original form of Christian faith, may be taken to be as comprehensively and simply stated as to satisfy the mind of the profoundest doctor of divinity or theological professor.

But even in his early days of narrow evangelicalism, he does not seem to have been fettered by any one special form of service. He tells us that he sat with much edification for a year or two under the ministry of Mr. Spurgeon; and while in Edinburgh he was an attentive listener to the glowing periods of Dr. Guthrie. Indeed, few men have attended the house of God more regularly than he. He says: "I am now sixty years old, and for forty-five of them was in church at least once on the Sunday—say once a month also in the afternoons. . . . When I am abroad, I am often in half a dozen churches in the course of a single day, and never lose a chance of listening to anything that is going on. Add the conversation pursued, not unearnestly, with every sort of reverend person I can get to talk to me— from the Bishop of Strasbourg, with whom I was studying

ecstatic paintings in the year 1850—down to the simplest
travelling tinker inclined Gospelwards, whom I perceive to
be sincere."

He is warm in his attachment to all animals and birds.
He has been seen to stop in Oxford streets to caress and
admire the dogs that chanced to cross his path; and those
who have read " Fors Clavigera " and " Love's Meinie "
know how passionately he has pleaded for the protection of the little birds that soar and sing in our English
sky.

Ruskin's generosity has been a lifelong characteristic.
His liberality at times appears to have approached prodigality
—gifts flowing forth in fifties, hundreds, and thousands of
pounds.   On one occasion when a young woman, who
had received brutal treatment from a man to whom she
was betrothed, was imprisoned because of her inability to
meet the recognisances of £40 enforced by the law owing
to her refusal to prosecute, Mr. Ruskin at once forwarded
the sum required for her release.   He has established and
endowed museums, dwelling-houses for the poor, and given
much of his money and treasures to the St. George's and
Oxford Schools of Art.   Discovering on his father's death
that he was sole inheritor of his immense fortune, he at once
distributed £7,000 among the relatives he deemed his father
to have overlooked.   Indeed, out of a fortune of £157,000
there remains but some £12,000, the rest having been distributed after the fashion named above.   At this generosity
the world laughs, deeming it foolishly and madly expended
money; whereas, if he had spent it in training horses rather
than in training men, it would have been set down as a mark

of his sanity, and he would have been enshrined as a saint of the turf.

John Ruskin was one of the band of men who set them-selves to carry out a system of education for the English artisan, and in connection with which the once famous Working Men's College was established in 1854. The principal was the late Rev. F. D. Maurice, and among the council of teachers were Thomas Hughes, J. M. Ludlow, and Dante Rossetti. Attendant at the classes was the now well-known George Allen of Sunnyside, who learned drawing under Rossetti and Ruskin. The college was eventually closed, having, as Ruskin says, "no head, but only a clasp to the strap of its waist, and as many heads as it had students." The apparent failure of the scheme led him to the conclusion that "the only proper school for workmen is of the work their fathers bred them to, under masters able to do better than any of their men, and with common principles of honesty and the fear of God, to guide the firm."

It is no easy matter to convey, especially in a paragraph, an intelligible and accurate outline of the intellectual and moral disposition of the man whose parentage, childhood, and manhood we have so hastily surveyed. His crowning mental gift is power of analysis; not the cold analysis of the scientific man of modern days, for linked to his analytical power is the wealth of a fervid imagination and a humble and reverent mind. Hence his penetrative glance detects the soul of things as well as their substance; and he re-members that when he sees most clearly he sees but through a glass darkly. He is a man of mighty heart; there beat within him passionate pulses ever keeping time to beauty in the world of matter, and to truth and righteousness in the world of man. When face to face with nature, fields and rivers, mountains and clouds, start wondrous music from his soul ; when face to face with man, craft and greed, falseness and death, call forth the " fierce lightning bolts " as of a "divine rage." In him is the spirit of chivalry : fearless when fronting or exposing wrong, he is tender as a child to all in weakness, sympathetic as a woman to all in pain.

Of John Ruskin's personal appearance little need be said. The photographers and engravers have made him so well known that even the busy crowds in our city streets are familiar with his face. I know of no faithfuller verbal portrait than that given by Mr. Smart in his inaugural address delivered before the Ruskin Society of Glasgow : "That spare, stooping figure, the rough-hewn kindly face, with its mobile, sensitive mouth, and clear deep eyes, so sweet and honest in repose, so keen and earnest and eloquent in debate."

CHAPTER II

EARLY LITERARY AND ARTISTIC EFFORTS.

THE beginnings of life are periods in which every moment trembles with destinies ; and the records of such periods, especially when those of the men who have faithfully and manfully fulfilled their course, are fraught with interest and profit. The aspirations of the youthful soul, the tentative work of early years, the wishes of parents, the advice of friends, the slow emergement from uncertainty into the one definite, infinite line of life—all these movements and their consequences can never be studied in vain.

Ruskin tells us in the "Stones of Venice" that God makes every man fit for his work ; by which he means that no man is without a divinely-appointed task, and a divinely-bestowed strength adequate for its fulfilment. His unwavering faith in this principle has been the source of his inspiration, and the fibre of his long-continued efforts. Man, with him, is not left to sink or swim upon a stormy sea as fate or chance may determine ; his life is rather the fulfilment of an appointed course ; and though he may not know its whence and whither, there is precious freight for his bark, a highway on the main for his voyaging, and a load-star that brings him to his desired haven. He holds life to be a Divine movement; and teaches us that He who so mysteriously originated and wonderfully fashioned man did not do so in vain. Nor does God spend His strength for naught; and we gather proofs of infinite purpose in man's being, from the infinite wisdom seen in his substance. Man's power of endless growth and his wealth of special endowment bespeak a Divinity seeking to shape and use; and testify that to some end was he born, and that for some cause came he into the world.

He who seeks his life's true calling must, according to Ruskin, seek it in the spirit of humility and patience— humility, enabling him to seek it in his own station, and that in the doing of little things rather than of great; and patience, to wait for the tide of fortune, once or oftener, rising in the lives of all.

With such humble and patient disposition there is to be the test of individual capacity by work—practice, and not speculation, being the revealing medium of power, and of its Divinely sanctioned channel. It is through continued effort and repeated failure that a man eventually discovers what he is, and what he ought to do; through this, alone, he attains the station in which he is most useful and happy, and secures the post and employment he was created to fulfil. The most distressful period in life—and likewise the most unsatisfactory—is the period in which a man feels the stirrings of his powers, yet sees no arena for their play; and the most miserable of men are those who, having missed their mission, find themselves on shipboard, bound for Tarshish, when their voice is needed in the streets of Nineveh. They are indeed unfortunate who thus find themselves at a work unsuited to their powers, and in circumstances unfitted to their calling. God never meant that it should be so. He who calls, fits; and He who fits, calls.

Ruskin's career is illustrative of his teaching; we see in it the frustration of the passionate wishes of his parents, and the accomplishment of a work other than the one suggested by his own early desires. His father and mother dedicated him to, and trained him for, the office of priest in the Established Church of England; and, to the last, they mourned their unfulfilled desires. But God had willed it otherwise. He called their son from the college halls of Oxford to prophesy in the temple of nature, ordaining him to minister at the altars of the everlasting hills. If John Ruskin had consulted merely selfish wishes, he would, no doubt, have given himself to artistic pursuits and travel, studying in the galleries of Italy, and occasionally exhibiting at the Academy; anon, spending his spare moments in the production of verse. But God qualified him for other work, and apprehended him for its accomplishment. Before, however, we look at the decisive step for ever fixing his future, it will be well to trace out some of those earlier movements and achievements which led him to forsake his parents' wish, for what he felt to be the Divine call of life.

We have seen how, from childhood, John Ruskin possessed the gift of taking delight in natural scenery; he likewise, from childhood, possessed the power of word-arrangement, both as to rhythm and accuracy. This unquestionable hint as to the direction in which the child's powers resided was recognised and wisely directed by his parents. They closely watched and carefully trained these first movements

of the youthful mind ; and, when scarcely nine years of age,
he rewarded them for their labour by composing the following lines, descriptive of a frosty day in Glen Farg, just north
of Loch Leven :

> " Papa, how pretty those icicles are,
>   That are seen so near,—that are seen so far ;
>   Those dropping waters that come from the rocks,
>   And many a hole, like the haunt of a fox.
>   That silvery stream that runs babbling along,
>   Making a murmuring, dancing song.
>   Those trees that stand waving upon the rock's side,
>   And men, that, like spectres, among them glide.
>   And waterfalls that are heard from far,
>   And come in sight when very near.
>   And the water-wheel that turns slowly round,
>   Grinding the corn that—requires to be ground—
>   And mountains at a distance seen,
>   And rivers winding through the plain.
>   And quarries with their craggy stones,
>   And the wind among them moans."

In this little poem we discover an accurate reading of
nature's forms and moods ; a delicate ear for the sound of
brook and waterfall ; a marvellous sequence in the arrangement of objects—icicles, dropping water, silvery streams,
trees, rocks, quarries ; and a weird-tone withal, the men,
spectre-like in the distance, and the wind moaning in its
winter haunts.   All this is worthy of note in the poem of a
child nine years old ; and in it we find part premise of his
future achievements.

Much of his time, during his earlier years, was spent in
wooing the muses.   He says : " A certain capacity for
rhythmic cadence (visible enough in all my later writings),

and the cheerfulness of a most protracted, but not foolishly indulged childhood, made me early a rhymester, and a shelf on the little cabinet beside which I am now writing is loaded with poetic effusions, which were the delight of my father and mother."

At the age of fifteen he was a contributor to a small periodical entitled " Friendship's Offering." These contributions took the form of verse; and though many bear the impress of the inexperienced hand, yet some are exceedingly fine. They are full of descriptive passages, and fairly glow with colour. In many of them we discover the writer's fondness for the sea, as, for example :

> " the breath-like pause and swell
> Of waters following in eternal fall,
> In azure waves that just betray,
> The music quivering in their spray,
> Beneath its seven-fold arch of day ;
> High in pale precipices hung
> The lifeless rocks of rigid marble rung,
> Waving the cedar crests along their brows sublime,
> Swift ocean heard beneath, and flung
> His tranced and trembling waves in measured time,
> Along his golden sands with faintly falling chime."

Or again, take the following description of a wreck :

> " Its masts of might, its sails so free,
> Had borne the scathless keel
> Through many a day of darkened sea,
> And many a storm of steel ;
> When all the winds were calm, it met
> (With home returning prore)
> With the lull
> Of the waves
> On a low lee shore."

Some of his river sketches are of equal beauty ; take these few lines from the poem entitled " The Broken Chain " :

" Along the Loire white sails are flashing,
    Through stars of spray their dark oars dashing ;
The rocks are reddening one by one,
The purple sand-banks flushed with sun,
And crowned with fire on crags and keep,
Amboise ! above thy lifted steep,
Far lightening o'er the subject vale,
Blaze thy broad range of ramparts pale !"

Now and again he gives us in these poems a powerful sketch of mountain scenery, as in the one entitled " The Hills of Carrara " :

" Far in the depth of voiceless skies,
    Where calm and cold the stars are strewed,
The peaks of pale Carrara rise,
    Nor sound of storm, nor whirlwind rude,
    Can break their chill of marble solitude ;
The crimson lightnings round their crest
    May hold their fiery feud—
They hear not, nor reply ; their chasméd rest
    No floweret decks, nor herbage green, nor breath
    Of moving thing can change their atmosphere of death."

But perhaps the most beautiful of these early poetic productions is the one entitled

"THE OLD WATER WHEEL.

" It lies beside the river ; where the marge
    Is dark with many a black and oarless barge ;
And yeasty filth, and leafage wild and rank,
Stagnate and batten by the crumbling bank.

Once, slow revolving by the industrious mill,
It murmured,—only on the Sabbath still ;
And evening winds its pulse-like beating bore,
Down the soft vale, and by the winding shore.

Sparkling around its orbéd motion flew,
With quick fresh fall, the drops of dashing dew ;
Through noon-tide heat that gentle rain was flung,
And verdant round the summer herbage sprung.

Now dancing light and sounding motion cease,
In these dark hours of cold continual peace ;
Through its black bars the unbroken moonlight flows,
And dry winds howl about its long repose,

And mouldering lichens creep, and mosses gray
Cling round its arms in gradual decay,
Amidst the hum of men—which doth not suit
That shadowy circle, motionless, and mute.

So by the sleep of many a human heart,
The crowd of men may bear their busy part,
Where withered, or forgotten, or subdued,
Its noisy passions have left solitude.

Ah ! little can they trace the hidden truth !
What waves have moved it in the vale of youth !
And little can its broken chords avow
How once they sounded.   All is silent now."

The above poem was written when the author was twenty-
one years of age.   I have transcribed it from an MS. copy in
the possession of a gentleman who was privileged to extract
it from a gift copy of John Ruskin's poems, lent to him by
Dr. John Brown, author of " Rab and his Friends."   The
doctor had underlined the second stanza with pencil.

Many of the poems reveal a depth of devotion, and a
spirituality of tone, which show his youth to have been lived
beneath the dominance of intense religious feeling.   In
proof of this the following lines on " Charitie " may be in-
stanced ; and it is to be hoped, ere long, they may find a
place in the hymnals of our land .

CHARITIE.

"The beams of morning are renewed,
  The valley laughs their light to see ;
And earth is bright with gratitude,
  And heaven with Charitie.

Oh, dew of heaven ; Oh, light of earth !
  Fain would our hearts be filled with thee,
Because nor darkness comes, nor death
  About the home of Charitie.

God guides the stars their wandering way,
  He seems to cast their courses free ;
But binds unto Himself for aye,
  And all their chains are Charitie.

When first He stretched the signéd zone,
  And heaped the hills, and barred the sea,
Then wisdom sat beside His throne,
  But His own word was Charitie.

And still, through every age and hour,
  Of things that were, and things that be,
Are breathed the presence and the power
  Of everlasting Charitie.

By noon and night, by sun and shower,
  By dews that fall and winds that flee,
On grove and field, on fold and flower,
  Is shed the peace of Charitie.

The violets light the lonely hill,
  The fruitful furrows load the lea ;
Man's heart alone is sterile still,
  For lack of lowly Charitie.

He walks a weary vale within,—
  No lamp of love in heart hath he ;
His steps are death, his thoughts are sin,
  For lack of gentle Charitie.

Daughter of heaven ! we dare not lift
   The dimness of our eyes to thee ;
Oh ! pure and God-descended gift !
   Oh ! spotless, perfect Charitie !

Yet forasmuch Thy brow is crossed
   With blood-drops from the deathful tree,
We take Thee for our only trust,
   Oh ! dying Charitie !

Ah ! Hope, Endurance, Faith—ye fail like death,
   But Love an everlasting crown receiveth ;
For she is Hope, and Fortitude and Faith,
   Who all things hopeth, beareth, and believeth."

These poems, the production of his childhood and youth, were printed, for private circulation, in the form of a small volume entitled " Poems, J. R. Collected 1850." Though their author saw fit to suppress them, they are, nevertheless, soon to reappear with additional poems hitherto unpublished. The precision of language, rhythm of metre, power of description, and love of colour, so manifest in all his later writing, are here already discoverable.

John Ruskin's earliest prose contributions were a series of articles on geology, written at the age of sixteen, and published in Loudon's Magazine of Natural History. These were followed by a series of essays for the Architectural Magazine, bearing the signature *Kata Phusin*. In an after-criticism on these latter he says, " They contain sentences nearly as well put together as any I have done since."

It was the first volume of " Modern Painters," however, that determined the future of John Ruskin. In its publication may be seen his initial step in the great field of art controversy. Hitherto he had fenced only, surrounded by friends, receiving from time to time their congratulations at the dexterity of his strokes, but now he has to front the un-sheathed steel of deadly foes, and war, single-handed, against the well-nigh unanimous verdict of his age.

It may be well to narrate here the history of the volume in the production of which he received his fire-baptism. Mr. Telford, his father's partner, gave him, when quite a child, a copy of Rogers' " Italy," illustrated by Turner. Child though he was, he intuitively read the beauty and caught the suggestiveness of Turner's vignettes. Indeed, so much was he absorbed in them, that when, on one occasion, he was introduced by Mr. Pringle to Rogers, he forgot to talk about the poems, taking up the whole of the interview in giving enthusiastic descriptions and searching criticisms of the engravings with which they were illustrated.

In this early acquaintance with Turner's art we discover the chief formative factor in his after-life. Henceforth he spared no pains to acquire a wider knowledge of the great painter's works ; and with such wider knowledge came an increased admiration and appreciation of his skill.

When Ruskin attained his majority, Turner would be somewhere between sixty and seventy years of age. He was then, if not at the meridian of his reputation, at the meridian of his power, and entering upon his third, and as Ruskin holds, his greatest period of work. In this advance he had risen high above the vulgar tastes of the nation ; consequently, having ceased to please it, its praise changed to scorn. Now that Turner was reaching his loftiest heights of thought, and manifesting a keener insight into the mysteries around him, pen and voice were alike lifted to proclaim what was deemed a waning power. It should be remembered that what is seldom seen is seen by few. Nature has her rarer moods, but these are seldom noticed or known by man. Turner, in the last period of his power, became alive to these rarer moods, and portrayed them with wondrous faithfulness. Inasmuch as he watched for those sunsets that but once or twice in twenty years throw their wealth of flaming colour over the western sky, and then, with matchless skill, revealed his sight to men, those who knew the setting sun only as oftenest seen, said he was false to nature, and attempting to " gild the gold of God." Inasmuch as his eye caught cloud-forms that are seldom seen in the life of man, and his mighty imaginative power ranged them upon the canvas, the men who knew but little of God's handiwork in the heavens spoke of these skies as faithless and gaudy. Inasmuch as he was lashed for hours to the mast of the tempest-ridden vessel in order to watch the waves clap their hands together, and hearken unto deep as it called unto deep, and thus catch the spirit of the storm, the miserable criticism of those who had never faced Nature in her moods of wildest energy, as they beheld his represen-tation, was " soapsuds and whitewash." Sight is propor-tioned to the power of the eye ; feeling to the depth of the soul. Here was a seer—a prophet of nature—telling his countrymen what he knew of the spirit of the universe ; and they in turn wagged their heads and mocked.

To one who, from youth, intuitively appreciated the genius of Turner, such criticisms were unbearable. They roused his soul from poetic reverie, and fired it for the fray. He plan of attack.   He wrote a lengthy letter in Turner's defence, purposing to forward it to one of the leading journals ; but, as it exceeded all journalistic limits, he threw it into the form of a somewhat bulky pamphlet, which continued to increase in matter until it finally shaped itself into the first volume of " Modern Painters."

Thus, at the age of four-and-twenty, John Ruskin challenged the verdict of his age concerning one of its greatest sons, and placed himself in direct antagonism to its standards of taste and estimates of truth.   At first, the country gazed in wonderment at the rashness of the attack —a youth defying the voice of a people, contradicting the criticism of its press, and asserting his art dicta in the face of the established canons of four hundred years.   When this surprise somewhat ceased, the whole affair was looked upon as the freak of one who had not cut his wisdom teeth, and it was sought to silence him with ridicule.   A critic, in " Blackwood," spoke of his style as excusable in a young curate's sermon during the first year of probation, and likely to win more nosegays and favours than golden opinions. But it was soon found that John Ruskin was equal to the warfare he felt himself called upon to wage ; and on the appearance of the second volume of " Modern Painters " his position as an art critic and prose writer was indisputable, and the throne of Turner for ever secure.

Little did Mr. Telford think when he presented a copy of Rogers' " Italy," illustrated by Turner, to the lonely child of Herne Hill, that in such act he was bestowing the key which was to unlock one of the most brilliant minds of its day. Yet it was even so.   Thus our greatest systems spring from small beginnings, and the thoughts of youth foretell the philosophies of after-years.

John Ruskin, in speaking of this period, says : " But the joyfullest days for me . . . . were in the triumphal Olympiad of years that followed the publication of the second volume of 'Modern Painters,' when Turner himself had given me his thanks ; to my father and mother his true friendship, and came always for *their* honour to keep my birthday with them ; the constant dinner party of the day remaining in its perfect chaplet from 1844 to 1850—Turner, Mr. Thomas Richmond, Mr. George Richmond, Samuel Prout, and Mr. Harrison."

Towards the close of the first volume of " Modern Painters," John Ruskin makes a special appeal to the young artists of England. He asks them to " go to Nature in all singleness of heart, and walk with her laboriously and trustingly, having no other thought but how best to penetrate her meaning ; rejecting nothing, neglecting nothing, and scorning nothing." A band of youthful and gifted painters responded to this call, chief among whom were Holman Hunt and John Everett Millais. The world met their efforts with a general guffaw, and pelted with mud the work they presented to its eye. The following is an extract from one of its criticisms : " These young artists have unfortunately become notorious by addicting themselves to an antiquated style, and an affected simplicity in painting. . . . We can extend no toleration to a mere senile imitation of the cramped style, false perspective, and crude colours of remote antiquity. We want not to see what Fuseli termed drapery snapped instead of folded, faces bloated into apoplexy, or extenuated to skeletons; colours borrowed from the jars in a druggist's shop, and expression forced into caricature. . . . That morbid infatuation which sacrifices truth, beauty, and genuine feeling to mere eccentricity, deserves no quarter at the hand of the public."

John Ruskin immediately took upon himself the defence of these young pre-Raphaelites. In a series of letters to the *Times* he points out the truthfulness of detail and the delicacy of finish in their works; and upholds them as faithful to their mission in drawing what they see, or what they suppose might have been the actual facts of the scene they represent; and pleads on their behalf for fair criticism, inasmuch as they then face a most critical period in their career—standing at a turning-point from which they may either sink into nothingness, or rise to very real greatness. During the year in which these letters appeared he published a pamphlet on pre-Raphaelitism, in which a further development of the defence of this school is instituted.

In all this early literary work he was carefully tutored and mercilessly criticised by the late Mr. W. H. Harrison, the editor of "Friendship's Offering," and a close friend of his father. He speaks of this gentleman as "my first editor," "my old literary master," and tells us how inexorable he was as to stops and grammar. In referring to the help he received from Mr. Harrison's supervision, he says : "Many a sentence in 'Modern Painters,' which I had thought quite beautiful, turned out after a forenoon's work, had to be turned outside in after all, and cut into the smallest pieces, and sewn up again, because he (Mr. Harrison) had found out that there was not a nominative in it, or a genitive, or a conjunction, or something else indispensable to a sentence's decent existence and position in life. . . . Not a book of mine, for good thirty years, but went, every word of it, under his careful eye twice over . . . often also the last revises left to his tender mercies altogether on condition he would not bother me more."

The time John Ruskin has been compelled to give to literature has necessarily limited his efforts in the realm of art. His first masters in drawing and painting were Harding and Copley Fielding; and throughout his life he has given many spare moments to the cultivation of their principles. He has illustrated his own works; and in the Walkley Museum, near Sheffield, many of his sketches may be seen. More than once he has exhibited at the Academy, and to-day he feels no little pleasure in showing to his friends, in a quiet hour, the productions of his brush. But it was as a prophet, not as a painter, that John Ruskin was to be known among his fellows: we have seen in this chapter how he was early called; in the following chapters we shall look at the nature of his mission—the burden of his words.

CHAPTER III.

JOHN RUSKIN is a genuine man of letters—a prophet in the realm of literature, fearlessly and unmistakably speaking forth the faith that is in him. The possession of a large private income frees him from the limitations so often imposed by publisher and public ; independent of both, he utters words impossible to those whose livelihood proceeds from the profits of their literary labours. In all his writings there is the free flow of conscience, mind, and heart. They possess a definite moral aim, and seek to rectify false national judgments, to condemn popular national sins, to restore well-nigh erased inscriptions of truth and beauty, and interpret the falsely judged and much maligned work of some of the world's greatest men. Few of Ruskin's co-temporaries in the realm of letters rival him in number of books issued, and few in range of subjects covered : more than forty volumes have already appeared from his pen ; while art, architecture, history, science, political economy, and the lighter fields of literature have in turn received his earnest thought and masterly exposition. It may be supposed that in writing so much, and upon so many subjects, he has of necessity written too much, and too superficially.

But it is not so: he proves himself an authority upon all subjects he takes in hand, and so treats them as to flood them with a fuller light, and clothe them in a more attractive garb.

His literary career may be divided into two main sections —the first dating from 1843 to 1860; the second from 1860, and continuing, with unabated vigour, up to within the last few years. The former embraces his great works on Art and Architecture, to the analysis of which the present chapter is devoted. The latter period, though embracing several series of art lectures delivered at Oxford, is mainly directed to a discussion of the principles of Political Economy and Social Science, an outline of which will be given in the succeeding chapter. These analyses will be the briefest possible—finger-posts set far apart, indicating for those who know little of Ruskin's teachings the track along which he journeys, and the wide and varied realms which he explores.

We have already referred to the events associated with, and giving rise to, "Modern Painters," and noted the fact that its five volumes cost their author over twenty years of labour. The first volume, which appeared in 1843, deals broadly with the general question proposed for discussion, and is divided into two parts. The first part sets forth a number of general principles, and the nature of ideas, conveyable by art—the greatest art being that which conveys to the mind of the spectator, by any means whatsoever, the greatest number of great ideas; and the greatest artist, he who embodies in the sum of his works the greatest number of such ideas. The ideas conveyable by art are

then enumerated and defined as follows : Ideas of Power,
or the perception or conception of the mental and bodily
powers by which the work has been produced, ranging from
the mere stroke of the finger to the workings of the most
exalted intellect. Ideas of Imitation, or the perception that
the thing produced is a resemblance only—the perfection
of such resemblances being that the imitation is never
mistaken for the thing imitated. Ideas of Truth, or the
perception of faithfulness in a statement of fact by the thing
produced—ideas of truth differing from ideas of imitation
inasmuch as truth treats of emotions, impressions and
thoughts, while imitation treats of material, rather than of
moral things. Ideas of Beauty, or the perception of beauty
either in the thing produced, or in what it suggests or
resembles ; such beauty being the subject of moral, and not
of intellectual perception. And, lastly, ideas of Relation,
or those ideas conveyable by art which are the subjects of
distinct intellectual action and perception, and worthy the
name of thoughts.

The second part of the first volume bears the heading :
" Of Truth," and is devoted to an application of the ideas
already considered. The order of application is : 1. The
truth of Tone, or the exact relief and relation of objects
against and to each other ; and the perfect relation of all
shades of them to the chief light of the picture, so that the
whole of the picture may be felt to be in one climate, under
one kind of light, and in one atmosphere. 2. The truth of
Colour, or the degree of accuracy in the artist's rendering of
the infinite and unapproachable variety of colour in nature.
3. The truth of Chiaroscuro, or the relation of nature's

4

shadows to her bright lights, and the proportion in which
she uses her highest lights and deepest shadows ; her lights
always being subdued if extensive, and her shadows feeble
if broad.   4. The truth of Space, as dependent upon the
focus of the eye, and the power of the eye to receive a clear
image of objects at a great distance from it.   The truth of
Skies is next discussed ; first, the open sky, then the clouds
in their cirrus, central, and rain cloud regions.   After which
follow several chapters devoted to the truth of Earth in its
general structure, its central mountains, and its inferior
mountains ; while lastly, the truth of Water is considered in
its manifold forms.   After thus stating the laws of truth in
the natural world, Ruskin shows, in a comparison of the
works of Turner with those of other artists, that Turner is
both more closely and more widely true to nature than any
of his fellows.

Having thus set forth in the first volume certain obvious
and *visible facts*, he proceeds in the second volume to consider the value and meaning of certain *mental impressions*.
The subject matter here, as before, falls into two main
divisions, dealing respectively with the Theoretic and
Imaginative faculties.   The Theoretic is distinguished from
the practical in science, as that which marks off the geolo-
gist from the miner, and in art the architect from the
builder ; and the mistake of applauding the practical to the
disparagement of the theoretical, with the disastrous results
consequent thereon, is exposed in a strikingly powerful
passage, which has become memorable in English literature,
on the Nebuchadnezzar curse.   The Theoretic faculty is
shown to be a moral, not a sensual or intellectual mode of

gratification ; and its special function, the sight and enjoyment of those beautiful qualities seen in the signature of
God upon His works.   The beauty thus revealed is arranged
under the divisions of Typical and Vital beauty ; the former
the type or resemblance of the Divine attributes, such as
Divine incomprehensibility in infinity, Divine comprehensiveness in unity, Divine permanence in repose, Divine
justice in symmetry, Divine energy in purity, and Divine
government by law in moderation ; while Vital beauty is
defined as the appearance of felicitous fulfilment of function
in living things, visible in the lower animals and in human
creatures when they worthily fulfil their offices.

Section II. discusses the Imaginative faculty in its three-
fold function of Association, Penetration, and Contemplation.
The Associative function is commandant ; summoning, re-
arranging, or removing as it pleases any group of images
which the mind may receive from nature : the Penetrative
function is analytic ; piercing at a glance to the heart of such
group, discovering its truth and loveliness, laying bare its
falsity and baseness ; while the Contemplative function is
regardant—the habit or mode in which the other functions
delight to work.

In the third volume Ruskin proceeds to examine the
success of artists, and especially of Turner, in the employment of these faculties ; endeavouring to discover who
among them has conveyed the noblest ideas of beauty, and
reached the deepest springs of truth.   The first question
discussed is the real nature of greatness of style.   This is
shown to consist of the four following features :—1. Choice
of noble subjects, indicating the artist's natural disposition

4—2

to dwell on the highest thoughts of which humanity is capable. Should, however, his subject be chosen for him, then his *treatment* of the subject is to become the test of his greatness. 2. Love of Beauty, such beauty to be ever consistent with truth ; not that the facts of ugliness are denied, but the artist does not delight to dwell upon them ; his passion going out towards the fairest forms, and insisting upon the beauty that is in them. 3. Sincerity, or the selection of the largest possible amount of truth in the most perfect possible harmony, the great artist choosing the most necessary truths first, and afterwards those most consistent with them. 4. Invention, or the treatment of facts imaginatively ; while lower art copies what is set before it, the higher art either imagines its subject, or so treats its subject as to manifest the three phases of imaginative power already explained.

Two chapters are then devoted to false ideals,—religious and profane. The origin of the latter is traced back to the falsity of the former, it being shown that when men sacrificed truth to beauty they abandoned the spiritual, and paved the way for the profane schools of art. Then follow a series of chapters on the true ideal as seen in the schools of the Purist, the Naturalist, and the Grotesque. Purism is unwillingness on the part of men of tender and holy disposition to contemplate various forms of definite evil necessarily occurring in the world ; such unwillingness indicating childishness of mind, and rendering true art impossible, inasmuch as pain and imperfection are eternally bound up with existence. Naturalism, occupying the central and highest branch of idealism, accepts both evil and good, taking straight from Nature its plain narration of fact, with this difference between the higher and lower artists, that the higher work from actual sight, or sight of faith, independently of all rules, and with instinctive truth, while the lower are, more or less, the slaves of rule.   The Grotesque, or allegorical, springs from the healthful but irrational play of the imagination in times of rest, from the irregular and accidental contemplation of things terrible or evil in general, and from the confusion of the imagination by the presence of truths which it cannot wholly grasp.

The latter part of this third volume is given to an analysis of Classic, Mediæval and Modern Landscape, as seen in the Greek, Italian and English mind.   The Greek mind is shown to be indifferent to the most striking scenes of natural beauty, its attention being turned to the beauty of human form and countenance.   The Mediæval mind delights much in garden solitude, and possesses an instinctive dread of mountains, from the fact that monks retired to them for penance, and hermits for meditation ; while the Modern mind revels in liberty, and lacks faith in the presence of Deity in nature.   We have as a result of these mental conditions, in Classic Landscape, natural surroundings subordinate to human use ; in the Mediæval, traces of solitude, piety, terror and superstition ; and in the Modern, cloud, mountain, and undue in   st in science.

The fourth volume gi   its opening chapters to a study of Turnerian Picturesque, Turnerian Topography, Turnerian Light, and Turnerian Mystery ; and, after a short study of the Firmament and Dry Land, enters into an exhaustive analysis of mountains.   First, the material of mountains is arranged in the order of " Compact Crystallines," "Slaty Crystallines," "Slaty Coherents," and "Compact Coherents "; then comes the Sculpture of Mountains—of the Lateral Ranges and the Central Peaks ; and, lastly, the Resultant Forms,—Aiguilles, Crests, Precipices, Banks, and Stones ; the volume concluding with two impressive chapters on " Mountain Gloom " and " Mountain Glory."

The fifth volume, after treating of the Earth-Veil of trees and flowers, and showing Turner's marvellous truthfulness in the delineation of all their forms and colours, closes with several striking chapters, in which are set forth the ruling ideas dwelt upon and expounded by the great artists of all ages ; with outlines of their birth, parentage, surroundings and teachers, tracing out in striking manner the effects of heredity and environment upon the work of their hands.

The " Seven Lamps of Architecture " appeared in 1849. This book owes its origin to certain facts discovered, and certain conclusions arrived at in the preparation of the third volume of " Modern Painters." It looks upon Architecture as the revealing medium or lamp through which flames a people's passions ; the embodiment of their polity, life, history and religious faith in temple and palace, mart and home. The first Lamp is Sacrifice, or the offering of precious things because they are precious, not because they are useful and necessary. When the spirit of sacrifice selects from two marbles it takes the more costly because it *is* the more costly ; when deciding between two kinds of ornament, it prefers the more elaborate because it *is* the more elaborate ;—such action being determined by the fact that in taking the more costly marble, and the more elaborate ornament, it can present in the same compass more value and thought. Ruskin distinguishes this spirit as unreasoning and enthusiastic, and negatively defines it as the opposite of the prevalent feeling of modern times which desires to produce the largest result at the least cost ; he also shows that the arts never flourish until primarily devoted to its service, and when so devoted give proof thereof, first in design, and then in expenditure.

Following the "Lamp of Sacrifice" is the "Lamp of Truth," or the spirit of reality and sincerity characteristic of all noble schools of Architecture. In the examination of this Lamp, Ruskin condemns, in no measured terms, all falsity of assertion in architectural construction, whether in nature of materials, quantity of labour, or substitution of effect for veracity ; and deems such untruthfulness deserving of the reprobation given to all other forms of moral delinquency. This insincerity is shown to be significant of the debasement of the arts, of a want of probity, and of a fatal separation between art and other subjects of the human intellect as matters of conscience. Architectural deceits are considered under three heads :—False suggestions as to mode of structure or support; false suggestions as to materials, and the substitution of cast or machine-made ornaments for those manufactured by hand. The downfall of art in Europe is then traced to the substitution of line for mass, and the abandonment of general principles of truth for those of mere expression and effect.

The third and fourth chapters set forth the Lamps of "Power" and "Beauty," or the expressions in architecture of the sublime and the delightful ;—the sublime, indicating man's power to *govern ;* the delightful, man's power to *gather.* Great buildings are viewed as displaying man in his governing and gathering capacities; his success being proportionate to his knowledge of how to govern and gather. Governing ability shows itself in *situation* and *line,* as seen in the natural surroundings chosen for vantage point and background, and the form into which the material is thrown ; the " Lamp of Power " revealing itself in the selection of grand natural eminences, and in shaping thereon structures after the model of the celestial city whose length, breadth, and height are equal. Gathering ability, as represented in the " Lamp of Beauty," is seen in *ornamentation ;*—the selection and arrangement of such ornament as will be effective, and characterised by truthfulness of resemblance to the varied types of beauty in the natural world.

Next is "The Lamp of Life," or the vividness of expression on the part of the intellectual power in its treatment of inert substances. It is the spirit that seizes upon substances, alike in use and outward form, and clothes them with its own nobleness, energy, and passion, until the rough-hewn stones are lifeful, and the veined marbles breathe. This Spirit of Life is distinguished from the spirit of death in its power to animate. The spirit of death may act, and imitate, but it is powerless to inspire. Life, in a word, is originality. Should the great architect imitate, his imitation is original, frank, and fearless; while the perfection of his work is not the perfection of execution where workmanship runs ahead of design, but the perfection of growth where design is ever ahead of workmanship.

The last two Lamps are those of " Memory," and " Obedience;" the former ever burning brightly and steadily among those people who reverence the past; flaming forth in public buildings commemorative of national achievements; and shedding its lustre in the erection and preservation of the homestead, the scene of the sorrows and joys of their family life; the latter revealing a conformity in architecture, as strict and minute and authoritative, as the laws which regulate their religion, policy, and social relations; distinct and general amid all accidents of character and circumstance. The writer's own words are as follows: "If there be any one condition which, in watching the progress of architecture, we see distinct and general; if, amidst the counter evidences of success attending opposite accidents of character and circumstance, any one conclusion may be constantly and indisputably drawn, it is this: that the architecture of a nation is great only when it is as universal and established as its language; and when provincial differences of style are nothing more than so many dialects."

A work in three volumes, entitled the "Stones of Venice," appeared in the years 1851 and 1853. It treats of the archæology and history of Venice, unfolding the causes of her strength and glory, of her downfall and decay. Its aim, to use the author's own words, is to show that the Gothic architecture of Venice had arisen out of, and indicated, a state of pure domestic faith, and national virtue; and its Renaissance architecture had arisen out of, and indicated, a state of concealed national infidelity, and domestic corruption.

The first volume, entitled "The Foundations," unfolds the principles of all noble building, and sets forth the virtues

of architecture as three-fold; the virtue of doing the thing it
was intended to do in the best way; the virtue of saying the
thing it was intended to say in the best words; and the
virtue of pleasing us by its presence, whatever it does or
says. Next, architecture is considered in its two great
divisions of Strength and Beauty; or, in other words, as
constructive and ornamental. Constructive architecture
treats of the wall, the roof, and the aperture; the history
and development of each being considered in its turn. The
wall is traced through the successive stages of wall-veil, base
and cornice,—the pier, with its respective base, shaft and
capital, growing out of wall division. The roof is treated in
its manifold forms and strengths, shaping itself according to
national taste and geographical situation; and the aperture
is followed up from the simple opening or perforation
exposed to storm and sunshine, to be filled in mullion and
strongly panelled door, porched, canopied, or balconied, as
the structure may require.

In the second section, which deals with architectural
beauty, or the ornamentation of the structure already considered, Ruskin insists upon obedience to three great laws;
the first, governing the *materials* for ornament; the second,
the *treatment* of ornament; the third, the *arrangement* of
ornament. The material for noble ornament is shown to be
the delight of man in the representation of the forms of
God's work; the treatment of ornament is his power to seize
and portray its essential elements; and the arrangement of
ornament the adaptation of its position to the eye, securing
for delicate carving a near range of vision, seeing that it is
not only lost by distance, but led thereby to produce worse

effect than rougher work.   The volume is prefaced with an outline of the history of the city and her Doges ; and concludes with a brilliant description of the drive by road from the gates of Padua, beneath elms and vine festoons, to Mestra, and thence, by gondola, along the dark waters to Venice.

The second and third volumes show how Venetian architecture was ever subject to the temper of the State, rising and receding with the growth of the moral and the immoral dispositions of the people.   The second volume, entitled " Sea Stories," is devoted to a study of the buildings marking the Byzantine and Gothic periods ; the one, characteristic of the earlier ; the other, of the crowning era of Venetian life.   The Byzantine School, transplanted from other shores somewhere about the eleventh century, is not viewed in its spirit so much as in its form, inasmuch as Ruskin had not the opportunity of studying the original structures on their native shores.   He devoted himself to St. Mark's as the best existent type of this school, and therefrom lays down the following distinguishing features of its architecture : In construction, Incrustation ; in outline, the Rounded Arch of varying size ; in ornamentation, Breadth and Life.   Incrustation, or the overlaying of bricks with costly material, grew out of the necessity of circumstances, the builders having scant access to quarries of precious stone.   Cost, and physical conditions, forced them to make most of the little marble they could command, and it became a question of either studding the masses of bricks with blocks, or else dividing the blocks into layers, and therewith covering the surface of the walls.   The latter was the method adopted ;

and as a consequence of this enforced incrustation the following became the leading characteristics of the school: 1. Plinths and cornices used for binding the armour, light and delicate. 2. Science of inner structure abandoned. 3. All shafts solid. 4. Shafts sometimes independent of the structure. 5. Shafts of varied size. 6. Decorations shallow in cutting. 7. The impression of the architecture not dependent on size.

Growing out of this Byzantine Architecture is the school known as Venetian Gothic. Ruskin's opportunities for studying its rise and growth in their original forms enabled him to enter into an analysis of the spirit, or temper of mind from which Gothic Architecture sprang. This he declares to be :—" Savageness, or rude wild strength ; Changefulness, or the result of the freedom springing forth from such wild strength ; Naturalism, or the love of the untrained mind for natural objects for their own sakes, and the effort to represent them frankly, unconstrained by artistic laws ; Grotesqueness, or the disposition which delights in fantastic, ludicrous, and sublime images ; Rigidity, or the peculiar energy which gives tension to movement, and stiffness to resistance ; and Redundancy, or the uncalculating bestowal of wealth to labour. All these features are shown to be characteristic of the Gothic workman, and discoverable in all his workmanship. It is no one or other of them that produces Gothic, " but their union in certain measures. Each one of them is found in many architectures besides Gothic ; but Gothic cannot exist where they are not found, or, at least, where their place is not in some way supplied."

The third volume, entitled " The Fall," is devoted to an

analysis of Renaissance Architecture, or that of Venetian decline. This era is divided into three periods, distinguished as the Early, the Roman, and the Grotesque, each marking a distinct phase of degeneracy in Venetian life. The architectural characteristic of the first period is an intemperate use of Gothic forms, and a formal rather than a vital imitation of the worst features of the Byzantine School ; such intemperance and formalism being a reflection of the spirit of the people. This Early Renaissance was followed by the weaker and more degenerate school of the Roman Renaissance, the ruling feelings of which were Pride of Science, Pride of State, Pride of System and Infidelity. Its architects confounded science and art, and failed to discover that the one had to do with the facts, the other with phenomena, and that reason and report were distinct from, and lower than, instinctive sight and feeling. They pandered to luxury and arrogance, and shaped for the selfish and proud Venetian colossal palaces with their accompanying corridors, pedestals and terraces. They became slaves to the letter that killeth, and sacrificed freedom for technicality, building according to childish rule rather than to noble law.

The last period of Venetian decline begot the architecture, styled by Ruskin, "Grotesque Renaissance." It was the outcome of an unscrupulous love of pleasure, and its features were the worst and basest of all preceding styles. It was characterized by apathy, mockery, and diseased and ungoverned imagination ; and with it closed the career of the architecture of Europe.

The "Stones of Venice" is prophetic in its tone, and it would be well for us as a people to take to heart its lessons.

A nation's history, though uninscribed by the historian's pen, is yet written more truthfully, more lastingly, on the deep wrought blocks of stone that tell of her domesticities, her manufactures, and her religion.   All great architecture is the exponent of national virtue, and all debased architecture the exponent of national vice and shame.

Other, and smaller works appeared from John Ruskin's pen during this first period of literary activity.   " The King of the Golden River," 1851, written for the entertainment of a child ; a pamphlet, entitled " Pre-Raphaelitism," 1851 ; a Series of Lectures on Architecture, 1853 ; a tract on " The Opening of the Crystal Palace ;" " The Elements of Drawing," 1857 ; and two Lectures on Art and its Application to Decoration and Manufacture," entitled "Two Paths," delivered in 1858, and published in 1859.   Such is a brief outline of the work accomplished during the first twenty years of Ruskin's manhood.

CHAPTER IV.

SECOND PERIOD OF LITERARY ACTIVITY.

THE two great sections into which we have separated the
writings of Ruskin were distinguished by a change of
subject rather than by a pause in activity. Such change,
however, was neither sudden nor unnatural ; it was simply
the further application to the great questions of Social
Science and Political Economy of the principles already
applied to Art and Architecture. The characteristic feature
in the teaching of Ruskin is his use of principles ; and as
all principles are permanent and universal, it was natural
that he should be led from a study of art to a study of architecture ; and from architecture, which is the embodiment of
a nation's moral temper, to the study of the great social and
political questions of national life. Society is a solidarity,
and all its varied movements are parts of an unbroken unity;
the laws lying at the root of any one of these movements
being representative of the laws that lie at the root of all.
Hence the teacher who works from principles is not restricted
in his studies to any one line of movement, but possesses a
key to all ; and Ruskin, in his mastery of the principles of
discovery, accumulation and distribution in the realm of art,
eminently qualified himself for their application to the realm

of social and economic life. Let any man sit down and carefully read "Modern Painters," "Stones of Venice," and "Seven Lamps of Architecture," and he will inevitably anticipate Ruskin's later writings : so broad are the truths they unfold, so far-reaching the conclusions they arrive at, that the reader finds himself unconsciously applying their principles to his own life and work, whatever the station of his life or the nature of his work may be. The politician will be led to test his laws by them, the clergyman the construction of his sermons, the tradesman the principles of his business transactions, and the artisan the character of his workmanship. The movement, then, from the earlier period to the later, is natural and inevitable ; and those who inquire what the greatest art critic in Europe can know of the principles of political economy betray in such inquiry their ignorance of the far-reaching interpretation of principles, and of the law of continuity which runs throughout society.

We may arrange this second period of literary activity under four divisions.

First.—Lectures delivered in various parts of England, and dealing with Social and Political Questions ; now arranged in volumes, and forming part of the revised series of Ruskin's works.

Second.—Articles originally contributed to magazines ; now collected in volumes entitled "Unto this Last," "Munera Pulveris," and "Time and Tide ;" also forming a part of the revised series of works.

Third.—A series of letters to working men entitled "Fors Clavigera," numbering some ninety-six parts, and complete in eight volumes.

Fourth.—Lectures delivered at Oxford during his terms of professorship, collected into five volumes, and likewise forming a part of his revised series of works.

During this period other works of a miscellaneous character have appeared from his pen, including treatises on Botany, Geology, Ornithology, as well as books on the Laws of Art and Prosody for the schools of St. George. But it will be necessary to restrict this chapter to the limits of the fourfold division before named.

1. Lectures delivered in various parts of England, and dealing with questions of social life and politics. A volume entitled "Sesame and Lilies" contains three lectures, the subjects of which are "Kings' Treasuries," "Queens' Gardens," and "The Mystery of Life." "Kings' Treasuries" are the stores of truth hidden away in the writings of the world's great men; and the aim of the lecture is to point out what to read, and how. "Queens' Gardens" treats of the true function and sphere of woman; and shows, from the collected teachings of the great and wise of every age, that such function is a guiding and not a determining one; and that the true place of woman is within her gates as "the centre of order, the balm of distress, and the mirror of beauty." "The Mystery of Life" is a study of those perplexing questions which grow out of the spectacles of great genius perishing uselessly, and of powers for good turned into channels of evil and destructiveness; and after viewing the brevity, the vanity, and the disappointment of much in life, it urges home upon us the great lesson that such mysteries simplify themselves only as we nobly strive to do our work, and follow in the wake of our appointed duty.

5

The " Crown of Wild Olive " contains lectures entitled
" Work," " Traffic," " War," and " The Future of England."
The lecture on " Work " unfolds the question of labour and
its relations, under the divisions of Work to Play, or the
difference between those who work and those who play;
Production to Consumption, or the difference between those
who produce the means of life and those who consume
them; Head to Hand, or the difference between those who
work with the head and those who work with the hand; and
Sense to Nonsense, or the difference between those who
work wisely and those who work foolishly. The lecture on
" Traffic " was delivered before the merchants of Bradford,
in response to an invitation to come down and advise with
them about their proposed Exchange. Its main drift is to
show that lectures on architecture will ever fail to give
nobility to the buildings of a people so long as the principles which govern their commercial and social life are lacking
in righteousness and truth. The subject of " War " is
viewed, first, in the light of exercise or play, or the relation
it bears to the classes who make it, not to the conscripts
who wage it; next it is considered as aggressive, or the
fruit of desire for dominion; and, lastly, as defensive.
" The Future of England " is a call upon the higher classes
to use their influence and give their time to the training of
those beneath them, who, it is shown, are prepared to look
up to and follow them, if they, as born leaders, will but do
their duty towards them.

   " The Queen of the Air " contains three lectures on Greek
Myths, or Athena in the Heavens, Athena in the Earth,
and Athena in the Heart. In the above lectures Ruskin

enters into the history of these myths, tracing them from their original sources, and following their stages of development, finally endeavouring to discover their meaning and significance for the England of to-day.   This meaning and significance is, that the Air is given us for our life, the Rain for our thirst and baptism, the Fire for our warmth, the Sun for our light, and the Earth for our meat and rest.

Two lectures on the " Political Economy of Art," delivered in Manchester, appeared in a small volume in 1867, and have since been included in Ruskin's revised series of works, under the title "A Joy for Ever."   The lectures treat of the laws of Discovery, Application, Accumulation, and Distribution of Art, and contain very valuable addenda in the form of notes.   In their re-published form they embrace other papers on " Education in Art," " Art Schools," and " Social Policy."

Ruskin soon grew dissatisfied with the work of a public lecturer.   He found out that people followed him simply to hear what he had to say and how he said it, and not from desire to be taught by him, or to practise what he endeavoured to enforce.   The excitement, too, told upon his health, and he eventually abandoned the rostrum for other and wider methods of communicating truth.   Nevertheless he has since occasionally lectured at the London Institution, but his appearances in public are now rare.

2. Contribution of articles to magazines and newspapers. In 1860 Ruskin contributed a series of essays to the "Cornhill Magazine," entitled " Unto this Last ;" but the outcry against them was so loud and fierce that the editor, a friend of Ruskin's, was compelled to prohibit the publica-

tion of anything further on this subject from his pen. The editor of " Fraser's Magazine " then wrote to Ruskin stating that he believed there was something in the theories which " Cornhill " had rejected, and offering to risk the admission into the periodical he represented of any further papers Ruskin might think fit to prepare. Hence, during 1862-3, Ruskin cautiously, and at intervals, forwarded a series of essays on the same subject as before ; but, unfortunately, the publisher now interfered, and the papers were again suppressed. These articles on Political Economy, which public and publisher raised their voice and fiat to suppress, have since appeared in two volumes, bearing the titles " Unto this Last," and " Munera Pulveris."

"Unto this Last" treats of the " Roots of Honour, or the responsibilities and duties of those called to fulfil all offices of national trust and service "; " Veins of Wealth," or the true sources of a nation's riches ; " Qui Judicatis Terram," or the right distribution of such riches ; and " Ad Valorem," or the definition of Value, Wealth, Price, and Produce. This work is in reality the central principle of Ruskin's system of Political Economy, and its keynote :—" Government and co-operation are in all things the laws of life ; anarchy and competition the laws of death." He claims to have put all his strength into its creation, holding that it contains the best of his workmanship, and the maturest of his thinkings.

"Munera Pulveris" originally appeared in the form of four essays, but in its present volume form it is divided into six chapters, treating respectively of Definitions, Store-keeping, Coin-keeping, Commerce, Government, and Mastership.

The chapter on Definitions specifies Wealth as dealing with the essential properties of things; Money as dealing with conditions of engagement and exchange; Riches as dealing with the due relations of men to each other in regard to material possession, and with the just laws of their association for purposes of labour. In the chapter on Store-keeping, the three following questions are considered :—The nature of the store, or the direction of a nation's labour for right production; the quantity of the store, or the relation of the quantity of any article to the need of the population; and the quantity of the store in relation to currency, or the proportion of the exchange or credit power among the people to the goods stored for exchange. Coin-keeping, or the charge of a country's currency, is defined as the regulation enabling any person presenting a commodity of tried worth in the public market to receive in exchange for it a document giving him claim to the return of its equivalent, in any place, at any time, and in any kind. Commerce is distinguished from currency, which conveys right of choice out of many things in exchange for one, as the agency by which the power of choice is obtained; while Government is considered in its relation to customs, laws, councils, and their enforcement. The last chapter on mastership is devoted to the duty of the commanding rich to the obeying poor, in the fulfilment of which duty the following laws are to be observed: 1. The production of *useful* things; 2. Useful things in the production of which the workman may lead a *healthy life;* 3. On the part of the Master *a right appropriation and distribution* of the things produced.

In 1867 Ruskin entered into a lengthy correspondence

with a working man named Thomas Dixon, of Sunderland.
This correspondence originated out of the agitation for
reform which was then rocking the country from north to
south.   It contains, as the writer says, in the plainest terms,
the substance of what he desired to say to the English
working men : " The Reform you desire may give you more
influence in Parliament; but your influence there will, of
course, be useless to you,—perhaps worse than useless,—
until you have wisely made up your minds as to what you
wish Parliament to do for you; and when you *have* made
up your minds about that, you will find, not only that you
can do it for yourselves, without the intervention of Parliament ; but that eventually nobody *but* yourselves can do it.
And to help you, as far as one of your old friends may, in so
making up your minds, such and such things are what it
seems to me you should ask for, and, moreover, strive for
with your heart and might."

The letters forming this correspondence dealt with Co-
operation, Contentment, Legislation, Expenditure, Entertainment, Dexterity, Festivity, Things written, Thanksgiving,
Wheat-sifting, Dictatorship, Episcopacy and Dukedom,
Trade Warrant, Percentage, Education, Marriage, Mastership, Land Tenure, Soldiership, Submission and Authority.
A better handbook for working men cannot be found, and
he who studies it carefully and, as far as lies in his power,
applies it to daily life, will find contentment in his lot and
happiness in his labour.

3.   " Fors Clavigera," or a series of letters to Working men,
complete in eight volumes.   On the 1st of January, 1871,
Ruskin commenced a monthly letter to the Working men

and Labourers of Great Britain under the title of "Fors Clavigera," which title implies that they may be controllers, not creators, of a three-fold power—a *force* which, if they use with *fortitude*, will establish for them their *fortune*. These letters were originally sold at 7d. per copy, but as they increased in bulk the price was raised to 10d., at which price they continued. They deal with all questions which concern the welfare of the country and her sons; and in them may be found, though apparently without plan, the perfected system of teaching Ruskin seeks to leave to the world. They are full of the wealth of one of the most cultured men of his age, the experience of fifty memorable years, the mature conclusions of a mind long trained to hard thinking, and the prophetic declarations of a man who has seen more deeply than most into the sins and follies of his time. Travel, History, Science, Philosophy, Literature, Biographical and Autobiographical incident are all brought into requisition, and made to supply their quota to the one great end—the edification of the English working man. No grade in our social rank is overlooked, for the term workman embraces those who use their heads, while the term labourer refers to those who use their hands. The Statesman, the Squire, the Clergyman, the Master, may all find laws as to their modes of living and relationship. These letters also contain the laws of Ruskin's ideal society known as the Guild of St. George, the aim of which is to gather on suitable estates healthful men and women who are prepared to fulfil the appointed tasks, and obey the communal regulations enforced by its masters. These laws of St. George are simple, and relate to labour, exchange, accumulation of

fortune, distribution of wealth, and the regulation of home and civic life. Not that Ruskin ever expects to see them universally adopted in his own land, but he is hopeful that they will be adopted by the coming generations who shall go forth to people the waste places of the earth. It has been said that the best of "Modern Painters" is reproduced in "Fors Clavigera." It may be so, but it takes altogether different forms, and is clothed in a plainer and directer phraseology.

4. Lectures delivered at Oxford during Ruskin's term of Professorship. These lectures fill five volumes, and commence with a series of papers on Art in its relation to Religion, Morals, and Use, and on Line, Colour, and Light. This, the first series, was delivered before the University in Hilary Term, 1870. In the Michaelmas Term of the same year six other lectures were delivered on the Elements of Sculpture in their relation to Idolatry, Imagination, Likeness, and Structure. They are collected into a volume entitled "Aratra Pentelici," or the Ploughs of Pentelicus, a mountain in Attica, rich in marble veins. In the Lent Term of 1872 ten other lectures were delivered on the relation of Natural Science to Art ; these appeared during the same year in volume-form under the title of "The Eagle's Nest." These lectures on the relation of Natural Science to Art were followed by a course on Wood and Metal engraving, in relation to the arts of Florence ; and treating also of the technics of engraving on wood and metal, as well as expounding the engraving of the German School as represented by Sandro Botticelli. The last published volume of Oxford lectures, delivered in the

Michaelmas Term of 1873, is entitled "Val d' Arno," and treats of the thirteenth century art in Pisa and Florence, the works of Niccolo and Giovanni Pisano being the main subject of the treatise. Ruskin re-commenced the publication of the Oxford lectures after his return to the Slade Professorship, and several are already in pamphlet form on the subject of Art in England as represented in the works of Rossetti, Burne-Jones, Sir F. Leighton, Kate Greenaway, and others.

This, and the previous chapter, by no means cover the whole of Ruskin's literary labours. The publication of pamphlets, the editing of art catalogues, the preparation of historic handbooks for the student traveller, and the constant war of correspondence waged for years in the columns of the "Times," the "Telegraph," and the "Pall Mall Gazette," have taxed his strength, and swallowed up many hours of his active life. As we look back at this labour-time, stretching over well-nigh half a century, we cannot but feel that John Ruskin has right well fulfilled the Hebrew preacher's command to do whatsoever his hand findeth to do with his might. Every subject he has grappled with has received his most honest and fearless thought; while every undertaking claiming his service has elicited the bestowal of his full energies and roused the inspiration of his mighty heart. In all his labours he has felt the burden of a duty, and been straitened until it was fulfilled. He gives us in his books the choicest of words in the most perfect of styles. His art criticisms and principles of architecture are widely accepted; and there are not a few thoughtful men who believe his systems of Social Science and Political

Economy will, in due time, win a greater respect from the body politic than they have to-day. He has had as many as seven books in the press at once, of which he says, "any one of them was enough to take up the remainder of my life." The following was the plan, now intercepted, which he had purposed to complete during the last decade of his life :—A History of Fifteenth Century Art ; An Analysis of Attic Art, fifth century B.C. ; Life of Turner, with analysis of Modern Landscape Art ; Life of Walter Scott, with analysis of Epic Art ; Life of Xenophon, with analysis of the general principles of Education ; Commentary on Hesiod, with final analysis of Political Economy ; and a general description of the Geology and Botany of the Alps.

CHAPTER V.

SOCIAL SCIENCE.

IT is proposed in this chapter to arrange as far as it is possible the manifold and scattered teachings of Ruskin on the questions of daily life in relation to the home, the mart, and the commonwealth. He has never seen his way to systematize these teachings by throwing them into popular form, or by ranging them collectively under respective divisions; they lie broadcast in all parts of his writings, often appearing where least expected, and re-stated, again and again, with ever-increasing directness and vigour. The reader must prepare himself to meet with much in them distasteful to his own views, and contravening his own practice; but, we must remember that the most helpful teachers are those who tell us what we do not know, who make us face the truth we wish to shun, and who enable us to accomplish that to which we have not yet attained. Ruskin's attitude towards all social questions is that of a reformer—a radical reformer—and the odium associating itself with his name is the odium ever associating itself with those who, axe in hand, mercilessly attack our self-blinded errors, and unsparingly lay bare our selfishness and sin. In a word, his teachings on Social Science may be termed a system of "thorough."

He holds that the great evil of life is three-fold, and sums it up as follows :—

First.—Man's ignorance of himself, and the existing state of things he has to do with.

Second.—Man's misery in himself, and the existing state of things he has to do with.

Third.—Man's inclination to let himself, and the existing state of things he has to do with, alone, at least in the way of correction.

To rectify these he would first of all have man set about knowing himself and his surroundings—knowledge of himself implying a knowledge of the cunning of his right hand, of the capabilities of his brain, and the excellences and ailments of his moral nature. Until these are manifest to him he will be uncertain as to his true calling—he will have no guarantee for success or happiness in his toil. If the initial steps of such self-knowledge have not been gained in early education, he must proceed at once to gain them for himself; if he has already received hints as to their nature, his next step must be to put them to proof by bringing them into actual play ; for only as a man finds out what he can do best, and in the doing of which he is at his best, does he discover his Divinely bestowed powers and his Divinely appointed task.

In speaking of this self-knowledge, Ruskin says :—"The first thing, then, a man has to do, if unhappily his parents or masters have not done it for him, is to find out what he is fit for. In which inquiry a man may be very safely guided by his likings, if he be not also guided by his pride. People usually reason in some such fashion as this : ' I don't seem quite fit for a head manager in the firm of ——— & Co., therefore, in all probability, I am fit to be Chancellor of the Exchequer.' Whereas, they ought rather to reason thus : ' I don't seem to be quite fit for head manager in the firm of ——— & Co., but I dare say I might do something in a small greengrocery business ; I used to be a good judge of pease'; that is to say, always trying lower instead of trying higher, until they find bottom : once well set on the firm ground, a man may build up by degrees, safely, instead of disturbing everyone in his neighbourhood by perpetual catastrophes."

As to laws for discovery of strength and weakness in the moral realm he is equally direct and suggestive :—" Make sure that however good you may be, you have faults ; that however dull you may be, you can find out what they are ; and that however slight they may be, you had better make some—not too painful, but patient—effort to get quit of them. . . . Now, therefore, see that no day passes in which you do not make yourself a somewhat better creature ; and in order to do that, find out, first, what you are now. Do not think vaguely about it ; take pen and paper, and write down as accurate a description of yourself as you can with the date to it. If you dare not do so, find out why you dare not, and try to get strength of heart enough to look yourself fairly in the face in mind as well as body. I do not doubt but that the mind is a less pleasant thing to look at than the face, and for that very reason it needs more looking at ; so always have two mirrors on your toilet table, and see that with proper care you dress the body and mind before them daily. After the dressing is once over, think no more about it."

Let these rules—plain and old-fashioned though they seem —be patiently and accurately followed, and ignorance of our physical, intellectual, and moral qualifications, as well as uncertainty as to our rightful callings and possible developments, will disappear. In the knowledge of ourselves we shall gain that self-dependent power which is the secret of true work, and that self-conscious weakness which is the secret of true growth. To miscalculate our powers is to be misguided and miserable in our occupations, and to be blind to our dispositions is to stagnate in the gloom of death.

Men, however, are not only to know themselves, but their knowledge is to extend to "the existing state of things they have to do with." Of such knowledge many may say, "It is too difficult—too painful for me;"—but no matter however difficult, it must be gained ; no matter however painful, it must be understood and taken to heart ; here, as elsewhere, ignorance is death. In order to possess this knowledge there must be fearlessness and sincerity of search ; an eye ever open, blinking no fact, and a heart ever sensitive, smarting beneath all forms of evil. Ruskin says the bishop must know "the history, from childhood, of every living soul in his diocese, and of its present state. Down in the back street, Bill and Nancy, knocking each other's teeth out ! Does the bishop know all about it ? Has he his eye upon them ? Has he *had* his eye upon them ? Can he circum-stantially explain to us how Bill got into the habit of beating Nancy about the head ? If he cannot, he is no bishop, though he had a mitre as high as Salisbury steeple ; he is no bishop,—he has no sight of things." The men of wealth must know something of those through whom their wealth is gained. The landlord, snugly housed amongst his estates,—knows he anything of his tenantry on the bleak moor side, or far away in the fog of the fen ;—knows he of the rows of crowded tenements in the city gloom, from which he draws his rents? The master—does he know his workpeople ; are they so many living souls in his sight, or merely flesh and blood factors in the production of his wealth ? Does he know them by name, is he acquainted with the condition of their several lots, can he tell you whether their homes are cleanly, their offspring healthy, their morals lofty or low ? And the working classes themselves—do they know, or do they care to know, of their own surroundings ; do they know why their employment is one of pain, and their pleasures marked by excess and brutality; why the key of many of life's treasures is taken from them, and the unequal share of life's burdens strapped upon their backs? Such knowledge Ruskin urges upon us ; he would have us all know the *existing state of things* we have to do with,—whether it be good, or whether it be evil,—for solely upon such knowledge rests the possibility of improvement and the possession of permanent happiness and peace.

Thus we must not leave the work of improvement solely to public measures, nor seek for happiness in spheres foreign to our own. Having gained a knowledge of ourselves and of our surroundings ; having discovered what we can do and what needs doing ; we must by patient and persistent use of cur powers — no matter how feeble, — and in our own sphere—no matter how deplorable,—set about the work of improvement ; happiness may then become something more than a far-off dream, and the way of our feet other

than a way of death. Ruskin, when speaking upon this
question says, " All effectual advancement towards the true
felicity of the human race must be by individual, not by
public effort. Certain general measures may aid, certain
revised laws guide such advancement, but the measure and
law which have first to be determined are those of each
man's home. We continually hear it recommended by
sagacious people to complaining neighbours (usually less
well placed in the world than themselves), that they should
'remain content in the station in which Providence has
placed them.' There are, perhaps, some circumstances in
life in which Providence has no intention that people *should*
be content. Nevertheless, the maxim is, on the whole, a
good one; but is peculiarly for home use. That your
neighbour should, or should not, remain content with *his*
position, is not your business; but it is very much your
business to remain content with your own. What is chiefly
needed in England at the present day is to show the
quantity of pleasure that may be obtained by a consistent,
well administered competence, modest, confessed, and
laborious. We need examples of people who, leaving
Heaven to decide whether they are to rise in the world,
decide for themselves whether they will be happy in it, and
have resolved to seek—not greater wealth, but simpler
pleasure; not higher fortune, but deeper felicity; making
the first of possessions self-possession : and honouring themselves in the harmless pride and calm pursuits of peace."

Thus we may best improve ourselves and our conditions
by labouring faithfully where Providence has placed us, and
at that which Providence has given us to do. It is seldom a

man improves himself—and it is always to the injury of those with whom his lot is cast—when he forcibly wrenches himself away from his own station, and seeks other and higher callings and surroundings. A man is not justified in forsaking his station because it is low; he ought rather to remain in it that he may improve it. The reason why the conditions of certain stations remain so unfavourable is owing to the withdrawal of those who, by remaining in them, would have improved them. The existing state of things in the station in which Providence puts a man has first claims upon him; a man's first duty, and, generally, a man's life duty, is to those nearest to him. Ruskin never wearies of reiterating this truth : Improve the existing state of things you have to do with; to improve them you must know them ; and as you improve them you will improve yourself, and become happy in yourself and in your surroundings. Knowledge of, improvement of, and happiness in ourselves and our surroundings—such is the keynote of Ruskin's system of Social Science.

Let us see how he would apply this principle to the home, the mart, and the commonwealth.

1. The relation between parent and child; or, the ideal home.

Ruskin would have all men secure a home; he tells them the first great essential condition in the domestic relation of life is to be the possessor of a substantial structure, becoming for many generations a remaining place for the good man and his descendants. He says : " The first—not the chief, but the first—piece of good work a man has to do is to find rest for himself : a place for the sole of his foot ; his house, or piece of Holy land ; and to *make* it so holy and happy, that if by chance he receive order to leave it, there may be bitter pain in obedience; and also that to his daughter there may yet one sorrowful sentence be spoken in her day of mirth, 'Forget also thy people, and thy father's house.'"

"But I mean to make money, and have a better and better house every ten years."

"Yes, I know you do.

"If you intend to keep that notion, I have no word more to say to you. Fare you—not well, for you cannot—but as you may.

"But if you have sense and feeling, determine what sort of a house will be fit for you ;—determine to work for it—to get it—and to die in it, if the Lord will."

"What sort of a house will be fit for me ?—but, of course, the biggest and finest will be fittest !"

"Again, so says the devil to you ; and if you believe him, he will find you fine lodgings enough,—for rent. But if you don't believe him, consider, I repeat, what sort of a house will be fit for you."

"Fit ?—but what do you mean by fit ?"

"I mean one that you can entirely enjoy and manage ; but which you will not be proud of, except as you make it charming in its modesty. If you are proud of it, it is *un*fit for you,—better than a man in your station of life can by simple and sustained exertion obtain ; and it should be rather under such quiet level than above. Ashesteil was entirely fit for Walter Scott, and Walter Scott was entirely happy there. Abbotsford was fit also for Sir Walter Scott, and had he been content with it, his had been a model life; but he would fain still add field to field, and died homeless.

". . . My father's house at Herne Hill was exactly fit for him and me. He left it for the larger one—Denmark Hill, and never had a quite happy day afterwards. It was not his fault; the house at Herne Hill was built on clay, and the doctor said he was not well there; also, I was his pride, and he wanted to have *me* in a better house,—a good father's cruellest, subtlest temptation."

Ruskin recommends that wherever possible men should build their houses on a scale proportionate to their earlier rather than to their latter conditions, so that such houses may record what they have been, and from what they have risen. He ridicules as purely modern and fallacious the idea that a house to be well built must necessarily be large and showy. He would neither have them mere sheltering shells of brick and stone, nor monuments of wealth and fashion; but homes, commensurate with station, ever growing radiant with past associations, and enriching beneath the "golden stain of time."

In such homes he would enthrone woman as queen, bidding her remember that if she be false the strength of her husband will fail, and the future of her children be dark. He holds that social redemption is wrought out by the wisdom and virtue of the wife and mother; that from her only can the husband draw his inspiration, the children their hope: "Woman's power is for rule, not for battle; and her intellect is not for invention or creation, but for sweet ordering, arrangement, and decision. She sees the qualities of things, their claims, and their places. Her great function is praise : she enters into no contest, but infallibly judges the crown of contest. By her office and place, she is protected from all danger and temptation. The man, in his rough work in open world, must encounter all peril and trial : to him, therefore, must be the failure, the offence, the inevitable error ; often he must be wounded, or subdued ; often misled ; and always hardened. But he guards the woman from all this ; within his house, as ruled by her, unless she herself has sought it, need enter no danger, no temptation, no cause of error or offence. This is the true nature of home—it is the place of Peace ; the shelter, not only from all injury, but from all terror, doubt, and division. In so far as it is not this, it is not home ; so far as the anxieties of the outer life penetrate into it, and the inconsistently-minded, unknown, unloved, or hostile society of the outer world is allowed by either hus-band or wife to cross the threshold, it ceases to be home ; it is then only a part of that outer world which you have roofed over, and lighted in. But so far as it is a sacred place, a vestal temple, a temple of the hearth watched over by Household Gods, before whose faces none may come but those whom they can receive with love ;—so far as it is this, and roof and fire are types only of a nobler shade and light, —shade as of the rock in a weary land, and light as of the Pharos in the stormy sea ;—so far it vindicates the name, and fulfils the praise, of Home.

"And wherever a true wife comes, this home is always round her. The stars only may be over her head ; the glow-worm in the night-cold grass may be the only fire at her foot ; but home is yet wherever she is ; and for a noble woman it stretches far round her, better than ceiled with cedar, or painted with vermilion, shedding its quiet light far, for those who else were homeless."

Inasmuch as the main outlines of Ruskin's system of Education will be considered in the following chapter, we need only say here that the relation between parent and child is to be one of closest confidence,—a confidence growing out of parental love and filial reverence. In writing to a gentleman who was endeavouring to combat the evils besetting the pathway of youth, he says :—" All that you have advised and exposed is wisely said and bravely told ; but no advice, no exposure will be of use until the right regulation exists again between the father and the mother and their son. To deserve his confidence, to keep it as the chief treasure committed in trust to them by God: to be the father his strength, the mother his sanctification, and both his chosen refuge, through all weakness, evil, danger, and amazement of his young life."

Every home is to be rich in sources of enjoyment ; no other spot is to be happier or more attractive. The shelves are to be stored with books, choice though few ; and the windows and garden plots planted with flowers. Part of the discipline is to consist in useful employment ; parents encouraging their children in the manufacture of home-made articles, whether for dress or household use. Acquirements gained through education, whether vocal, artistic, or mechanical, are to minister in the spare moments of the day to the sick, the destitute, and the ignorant, parent and child ever remembering that out of idleness and cruelty spring those evils which darken the lives and destroy the hopes of the race, while in usefulness and quiet joy is found the secret of a nation's prosperity, and the root of a people's honour.

The peace of the household is somewhat dependent upon the amicability of relation between mistress and maid. Indeed, the question of domestic service is one which every true housewife must have pondered for long, oftentimes in the spirit of despair. The social system of Ruskin, leaving no corner unexplored, deals fearlessly and practically with this vexed, and well-nigh hopeless, question. He says:

" There are broadly two ways of making good servants; the first, a sound, wholesome, thorough-going slavery— which was the heathen way, and no bad one neither, provided you understand that to make real 'slaves' you must make yourself a real 'master' (which is not easy). The second is the Christian's way : ' whoso delicately bringeth up his servant from a child, shall have him become his son at the last.' And as few people want their servants to become their sons, this is not a way to their liking. So that, neither having courage or self-discipline enough on the one hand to make themselves nobly dominant after the heathen fashion, nor tenderness of justice enough to make themselves nobly protective enough after the Christian; the present public thinks to manufacture servants bodily out of powder and hay-stuffing—mentally by early instillation of Catechism and other mechanico-religious appliances, and economically by the law of supply and demand.

" There is only one way to have good servants; that is, to be worthy of being well served. All nature and all humanity will serve a good master, and rebel against an ignoble one.

And there is no surer test of the quality of a nation than the quality of its servants, for they are their masters' shadows, and distort their faults in a flattened mimicry."

The concluding sentence goes a long way toward a solution of this great domestic difficulty. Let every house-wife see to it that she is worthy of being well served; let her see to it that her children, too, make themselves worthy of service, and complaint as to the impudence of domestics will become a thing of the past. Let the housewife also see to it that she has a knowledge of the household—a practical knowledge—as the captain of his ship, and such knowledge will win for her respect and obedience on the part of those whom she employs. Is it not a suggestive fact that we find, from the biographies of our worthiest men and women, that they changed servants seldom, and that those who thus served them loved them as with their own life.

2. The relation of master to servant; or, the laws of labour.

The first great responsibility of the master, whether in agriculture, architecture or manufacture, is the life of the workman; and the next, the production of useful and durable work, and this for work's sake rather than for mere monetary returns. "The master becomes necessarily, in the course of his business, the overseer and governor of large masses of men in a most direct way, so that upon him falls, in a great part, the responsibility for the kind of life they lead; and it becomes his duty, not only to be always con-sidering how to produce what he sells in the purest and cheapest forms, but how to make the various employments involved in the production, or transference of it, most beneficial to the men employed."

Ruskin holds that all employments which simply task the workman as a machine are destructive of skill and degrading to manhood, and that in proportion to such destruction and degradation will be inferiority of work. He abhors the severance of thought from labour; and instead of setting one to think and another to execute, he would have thought and execution developed in the same man. Thus the workman's toil would be relieved from drudgery, and such relief, he believes, would advance excellency of workmanship and beget a more kindly feeling between master and man. Until labourers have a zest in their labour their labour will be in vain, and there can be little doubt that the substitution of machinery for hand-made labour, and the monotony of employment necessitated thereby, have done much to kill enthusiasm and cripple skill. Let the following weighty words be marked: "Now, in the make and nature of every man, however rude or simple, whom we employ in manual labour, there are some powers for better things: some tardy imagination, torpid capacity of emotion, tottering steps of thought, there are, even at the worst; and in most cases it is all our own fault that they *are* tardy or torpid. But they cannot be strengthened, unless we are content to take them in their feebleness, and unless we prize and honour them in their imperfection above the best and most perfect manual skill. And this is what we have to do with all our labourers, to look for the *thoughtful* part of them, and get that out of them, whatever we lose for it, whatever faults and errors we are obliged to take with it. For the best that is in them cannot manifest itself, but in company with much error. Understand this clearly : You can teach a man to draw a straight line, and to cut one ; to strike a curved line, and to carve it ; to copy and carve any number of given lines or forms, with admirable speed and perfect precision ; and you find his work perfect of its kind ; but if you ask him to think about any of those forms, to consider if he cannot find any better in his own head, he stops ; his execution becomes hesitating ; he thinks, and ten to one he thinks wrong ; ten to one he makes a mistake in the first touch he gives to his work as a thinking being. But you have made a man of him for all that. He was only a machine before, an animated tool.

"And observe, you are put to stern choice in this matter. You must either make a tool of the creature, or a man of him. You cannot make both. Men were not intended to work with the accuracy of tools, to be precise and perfect in all their actions. If you will have that precision out of them, and make their fingers measure degrees like cogwheels, and their arms strike curves like compasses, you must unhumanize them. All the energy of their spirits must be given to make cogs and compasses of themselves. All their attention and strength must go to the accomplishment of the mean act. The eye of the soul must be bent upon the finger point, and the soul's force must fill all the invisible nerves that guide it, ten hours a day, that it may not err from its steely precision, and so soul and sight be worn away, and the whole human being be lost at last—a heap of sawdust, so far as its intellectual work in this world is concerned; saved only by its Heart, which cannot go into the forms of cogs and compasses, but expands after the ten hours are over, into fireside humanity. . . . It is verily this degradation of the operative into a machine, which, more than any other evil of the times, is leading the mass of the nations everywhere into vain, incoherent, destructive struggling for a freedom of which they cannot explain the nature to themselves. Their universal outcry against wealth, and against nobility, is not forced from them either by the pressure of famine, or the sting of mortified pride. These do much, and have done much in all ages; but the foundations of society were never yet shaken as they are to-day. It is not that men are ill fed, but that they have no pleasure in the work by which they make their bread, and therefore look to wealth as the only means of pleasure. . . . We have much studied and much perfected, of late, the civilized invention of the division of labour; only we give it a false name. It is not, truly speaking, the labour that is divided; but the men: Divided into mere segments of men—broken into small fragments and crumbs of life; so that all the little piece of intelligence that is left in a man is not enough to make a pin, or a nail, but exhausts itself in making the point of a pin, or the head of a nail. Now it is a good and desirable thing, truly, to make many pins in a day; but if we could only see with what crystal sand their points were polished—sand of human soul, much to be magnified before it can be discerned for what it is—we should think there might be some loss in it also. And the great cry that rises from all our manufacturing cities, louder than their furnace blast, is all in very deed for this—that we manufacture everything there except men ; we blanch cotton, and strengthen steel, and refine sugar, and shape pottery ; but to brighten, to strengthen, to refine, or to form a single living spirit, never enters into our estimate of advantages. And all the evil to which that cry is urging our myriads can be met only in one way : not by teaching nor preaching, for to teach them is but to show them their misery, and to preach to them, if we do nothing more than preach, is to mock at it. It can be met only by a right understanding, on the part of all classes, of what kinds of labour are good for men, raising them, and making them happy ; by a determined sacrifice of such convenience, or beauty, or cheapness, as is to be got only by the degradation of the workman ; and by equally determined demand for the products and results of healthy and ennobling labour."

This lengthy extract will give the reader the gist of Ruskin's position on machine-made *versus* hand-made work, and explain his views as to the detrimental effects of the so-called " division of labour," which he denounces as the division of men.

Not that he would exclude all machine labour, nor even altogether prohibit steam power ; his antagonism is to the *labour* that kills, and to the unlimited multiplication of machinery which leads to the enforced idleness and deterioration of the workman. He inquires how many thousands of pairs of hands are useless, how many thousands of able-bodied men are idle because no man hath called them ? He would use all this muscle-force ere he utilized the forces of nature : gathering his countrymen into ranks and communities, he would train and set them to pleasing and useful toil until there were none idle save the dead. Then he would appropriate the forces of nature, storing the waters now wasted in the rainy seasons, deepening the beds of rivers, catching the winds in sails of mill and ship, to give power to the factory and speed to commerce. And if the demand was still greater than could be met by this combination of trained muscle and nature force, he would erect furnaces, and build chimneys, and run steamships; but even then not at the expense of turning workmen into machines, nor of the destruction of their cunning through the severity and inhumanity of toil. His own words are these: " The general principles by which employment should be regulated may be briefly stated as--vital or muscular power; natural mechanical power of wind, water, and electricity; and artificially produced mechanical power; it is the first principle of economy to use all available vital power first, then the inexpensive natural forces, and only at last to have recourse to artificial power. And this, because it is always better for a man with his own hands to feed and clothe himself, than to stand idle while a machine works for him, and if he cannot by all the labour healthily possible to him feed and clothe himself, then it is better to use an inexpensive machine—as a windmill or water-mill—than a costly one like a steam-engine, so long as we have natural force enough at our disposal."

Ruskin's views as to the question of wages have created much discussion, and not a little angry feeling on the part of the employers of labour. He holds that work and wages practically mean the food and lodging given to the workers by the possessors of the soil; and while he would raise the labourer above the standard which simply works for pay, yet he would have no man underpaid, nor would he employ men at a labour destructive to their manhood His two central principles as to returns for time and strength given in the production of commodities are, that a man should be paid according to his skill, and risks of all kinds be taken into due consideration. The following are his words:—

"I.—A man should in justice be paid for two hours' work twice as much as for one hour's work, and for n hours' work n times as much, if the effort be similar and continuous.

"II.—A man should in justice be paid for difficult or dangerous work proportionately more than for easy and safe work, supposing the other conditions of the work similar.

"III.—If a man does a given quantity of work for me, I am bound in justice to do, or procure to be done, a precisely equal quantity of work for him; and just trade in labour is the exchange of equivalent quantities of labour of different kinds."

As to method of payment he is equally clear and practical. "The quantity of food and air which will enable a man to perform a piece of labour without eventually losing any of his flesh and nervous energy, is as absolutely fixed a quantity as the weight of powder necessary to carry a given ball a given distance. . . . . Let any half-dozen London physicians, of recognised standing, state in precise terms the quantity and kind of food and space of lodging necessary for the healthy life of a labourer in any given manufacture, and the number of hours he may, without shortening his life, work at such business daily, if in such manner he be sustained.

Let all masters be bound to give their men a choice between
an order for that quantity of food and space of lodging, or
the market wages for the specific number of hours of
work. Proper laws for the maintenance of families would
require further concession; but in the outset, let but this
law of wages be established, and if then we have more
strikes, you may denounce them without one word of re-
monstrance either from sense or sensibility."

All remuneration, regardless of the life of the workman,
falls below Ruskin's standard of wage. Pay your men
according to their skill; consider the risk they run in your
employ; and see to it that the poorest receive that which
embraces healthful surroundings and supplies the necessary
demands of life.

Further, Ruskin reminds the merchant and manufacturer
of their obligations to the public: they are the servants of
the nation and exist for its welfare. Just as it is the duty
of a soldier to defend a nation, of a pastor to teach it, of a
physician to keep it in health, and of a lawyer to enforce
justice in it; so is it the duty of a merchant and manufacturer to provide for it. In all these callings there is a
vital responsibility, a sacred trust; and upon a consciousness of such responsibility, together with its faithful fulfilment, depends the soundness and prosperity of all national
life. No temptation, however subtle; no trial, however
terrible; must move from their duty the men who fill these
posts of honour and of trust. The soldier must die rather
than forsake the ranks; the pastor starve rather than preach
with flattering tongue; the physician risk the deadliest
disease rather than fly from plague; the lawyer sacrifice

brief and fee rather than countenance injustice ; and the merchant and manufacturer suffer bankruptcy and beggary rather than adulterate their provisions, manufacture shoddy stuffs, or provide for the public inadequate or destructive material.

He says :—" A good soldier, for instance, mainly wishes to do his fighting well. He is glad of his pay—very properly so, and justly grumbles when you keep him ten years without it—still, his main notion of life is to win battles, not to be paid for winning them. So of clergymen. They like pew-rents, and baptismal fees, of course ; but yet, if they are brave and well educated, the pew-rent is not the sole object of their lives, and the baptismal fee is not the sole purpose of their baptism ; the clergyman's object is essentially to baptize and preach, not to be paid for preaching.

" So of doctors. They like fees, no doubt—ought to like them ; yet if they are brave and well-educated, the entire object of their lives is not fees. They, on the whole, desire to cure the sick ; and, if they are good doctors, and the choice were fairly put to them, would rather cure their patient, and lose their fee, than kill him, and get it. And so with all other brave and rightly trained men ; their work is first, their fee is second. Very important always, but still *second*. But in every nation, as I said, there are a vast class who are ill-educated, cowardly, and more or less stupid. And with these people, just as certainly the fee is first, and the work second, as with brave people the work is first and the fee second. And this is no small distinction. It is the whole distinction in a man : distinction between life and death *in* him, between heaven and hell *for* him. You cannot serve two masters; you must serve one or other. If your work is first with you, and your fee second, work is your master, and the lord of work, who is God. But if your fee is first with you, and your work second, fee is your master, and the lord of fee, who is the devil."

With the brave and rightly trained merchant and manufacturer who realize the vital functions of their calling, and the responsibility growing therefrom, fee is never first; they feel that independently of profits—at all costs—they must be faithful to the nation whose they are and whom they serve: in other words, they are prepared to turn out good work or die. And such men are conscious that in palming off an adulterated article they are as culpable as any soldier who runs to lessen risk, or any preacher who lies to retain his church.

3. Relations between governors and governed; or, the laws of commonwealth.

With his great master, Carlyle, Ruskin holds that a nation's divinely appointed leaders are found in her greatest and wisest men; such men, in the evolution of national life, coming to the fore, and being for some little time, at least, within the reach of a people's choice. Then it is that a wise people secures them; and having secured them, silently obeys them. This power of wise choice, and this spirit of faithful obedience, is the outcome of prior discipline, obedience in the subject ever being promotive of advancement in the law. "Learn to obey good laws, and in a little while you will reach the better learning—how to obey good men, who are living, breathing, unblinded law."

The laws Ruskin enforces in St. George's Guild, and

hence, we may conclude, the laws he would have us as a nation adopt, are those of Florence in the fourteenth century, with certain modifications necessitated by the lapse of five hundred years. They are largely communal, and have to do with the health and education of the people, with supply and demand, and with the accumulation and distribution of wealth. Applied to our own nation they would lay hold of every man, woman, and child, as members of state, and train, and compel them to follow the work for which nature and education fitted them ; they would dispense a people's meat and raiment, providing healthful meat, purchasable at a normal price, and clothing serviceable in texture and beautiful in shape and hue ; they would remove the nation's coinage from out the hands of a few prosperous traffickers, and her lands from under the monopoly of those of favoured birth, placing the coinage and wealth in the nation's hands for the nation's use—public buildings being the costliest, public treasures the rarest, public lands the most spacious and beautiful ; they would enforce the construction of streets in the form of squares, every house being well built and skilfully designed ; and they would prohibit the walls of any city enclosing more than five and twenty thousand souls ; the law of life observed would be that of co-operation—not the co-operation of a privileged number of persons for their own selfishness, but the co-operation of all for the good of one another ; while the creed which they would seek to develop in each human being whose life they sought to regulate would be :

"I.—I trust in the living God, Father Almighty, Maker

7

of Heaven and Earth, and of all things and creatures, visible and invisible.   I trust in the kindness of His law, and the goodness of His work.   And I will strive to love Him and to keep His law, and to see His work while I live.

"II.—I trust in the nobleness of human nature—in the majesty of its faculties, the fulness of its mercy, and the joy of its love.   And I will strive to love my neighbour as myself, and even when I cannot, I will act as if I did.

"III.—I will labour, with such strength and opportunity as God gives me, for my own daily bread; and all that my hand finds to do, I will do it with my might.

"IV.—I will not deceive, or cause to be deceived, any human being for my gain or pleasure; nor hurt, nor cause to be hurt, any human being for my gain or pleasure; nor rob, nor cause to be robbed, any human being for my gain or pleasure.

"V.—I will not kill nor hurt any living creature needlessly, nor destroy any beautiful thing; but will strive to save and to comfort all gentle life, and guard and perfect all natural beauty upon the earth.

"VI.—I will strive to raise my own body and soul daily into higher powers of duty and happiness; not in rivalship or contention with others, but for the help, delight, and honour of others, and for the joy and peace of my own life.

"VII.—I will obey all the laws of my country faithfully; and the orders of its monarch, so far as such laws and commands are consistent with what I suppose to be the law of God; and when they are not so, or seem in any wise to need change, I will oppose them loyally and deliberately—not with malicious, concealed, or disorderly violence.

"VIII.—And with the same faithfulness, and under the limits of the same obedience, which I render to the laws of my country, and the commands of its rulers, I will obey the laws of the society called of St. George . . . . and the order of its masters, and of all persons appointed to be in authority under its masters, so long as I remain a companion called of St. George."

CHAPTER VI.

EDUCATION.

EDUCATION seeks to discover and develop the innate powers of child life; its work is to educe as well as to instil, to draw forth the actual from out the possible, as well as to train the actual to shapeliness and use. In all true systems of education, development and equipment accompany each other, the child not only being furnished with the implements required in its future life, but receiving, at the same time, a knowledge of *how* to use them rightly, and *where* to use them to the best of purpose for itself and others. There is a knowledge which is destructive as well as a knowledge which is edifying; and to be in possession of facts and theories, to be vested with strength and influence, and yet ignorant withal of their rightful aim and governance, is to be in possession of a dangerous, if not a fatal force. "An educated man," says Ruskin, "is one who has understanding of his own uses and duties in the world, and, therefore, of the general nature of the things done and existing in the world; and who has so trained himself, or been trained, as to turn to the best and most courteous account whatever faculties or knowledge he has." Thus, the great end of education is to get out of the child its possibilities, and so to train them as to enable it to use them in the best possible manner, in the station and at the work to which it is called.

To this great end Ruskin would start with the child in the first stages of its infant life. He asks : " When do you suppose the education of a child begins ? At six months old it can answer smile with smile, and impatience with impatience. It can observe, enjoy, and suffer acutely, and, in a measure, intelligently. Do you suppose it makes no difference to it that the order of the house is perfect and quiet, the faces of its father and mother full of peace, their soft voices familiar to its ear, and even those of strangers, loving ; or that it is tossed from arm to arm, among hard, or reckless, or vain-minded persons, in the gloom of a vicious household, or the confusion of a gay one ? The moral disposition is, I doubt not, greatly determined in those first speechless years. I believe especially that quiet, and the withdrawal of objects likely to distract, by amusing, the child, so as to let it fix its attention undisturbed on every visible least thing in its domain, is essential to the formation of some of the best powers of thought."

Few parents realize that the crystallization of child character is progressing in these first speechless years, that every look and sound leave their impress long ere they can be translated by the maturer intelligence of the child. As to what the surroundings of child life are to be, as far as it is possible to secure them, the following letter will show :

" BRANTWOOD, CONISTON, LANCASHIRE,
"23rd *November*, 1881.

" MY DEAR ———,

" I have never written a pamphlet on nurseries ; first, because I never write about anything except what I know more of than most other people ; secondly, because I think nothing much matters in a nursery—except the mother, the nurse, and the air.

"So far as I have any notion or guess in the matter myself, beyond the perfection of those three necessary elements, I should say, the rougher and plainer everything the better— no lace to cradle cap, hardest possible bed and simplest possible food according to age, and floor and walls of the cleanablest.

"All education to beauty is first—in the beauty of gentle human faces round a child; secondly, in the fields—fields meaning, 'grass, water, beasts, flowers, and sky.'

"Without these, no man can be educated humanly. He may be made a calculating machine—a walking dictionary— a painter of dead bodies—a twangler or scratcher on keys or cat-gut—a discoverer of new forms of worms in mud. But a properly so-called human being—never.

"Pictures are, *I believe*, of no use whatever by themselves. If the child has other things right, round it, and given to it, —its garden, its cat, and its window to the sky and stars,-· in time, pictures of flowers, and beasts, and things in Heaven, and Heavenly earth, may be useful to it. But see first that its realities are heavenly.

"I am, etc.,

"J. RUSKIN."

The surroundings recommended by Ruskin in this letter will be seen, by reference to a previous chapter, to be mainly the surroundings of his own childhood; and truly we cannot have a better proof of their value than their effect upon his own life. The sights and sounds of our crowded towns and cities, of our smoke-stained villages and blackened heaths, are destructive to health and heart of child-life. The strongest soul is dependent upon environment; early associations are life-long factors in the character of the greatest men. If the child is father to the man, and if environment is no mean factor in the shaping of the child, there is depth of meaning in the closing sentence of this letter:—"See first that its surroundings are heavenly."

He is equally clear and suggestive when he treats of the training in youth, denominated by him the forming time, in which a man makes himself, or is made, what he is for ever. In the appendix to the fourth volume of "Modern Painters" is the following striking passage:—"The whole period of youth is one essentially of formation, edification, instruction —I use these words with their weight in them; intaking of stores, establishment in vital habits, hopes, faiths. There is not an hour of it but it is trembling with destinies, not a moment of which, once passed, the appointed work can ever be done again, or the neglected blow struck on the cold iron. Take your vase of Venice glass out of the furnace, and strew chaff over it in its transparent heat, and recover that to its clearness and rubied glory when the north wind has blown upon it: but do not think to strew chaff over the child fresh from God's presence, and to bring the heavenly colours back to him—at least in this world."

Are not these the words of a prophet who is seeking to turn the hearts of the fathers to their children? There is no diviner gift than life—no weightier responsibility than parentage. Our children come bright from God's presence radiant with the light of Heaven, His latest revelation of Himself to our care-hardened lives. Do we treasure the lessons they teach; do we seek to retain the glory they reveal? Are we nursing the divine germ for fuller development, and taking heed lest in word or deed we offend these little ones whose angels behold the face of their Father which is in heaven? These questions lie at the root of all education, and Ruskin never wearies of driving them home.

From environment he passes to the cultivation of the body. Strength, and beauty of physique, are to be sought through discipline; and for this end schools are to be established in open spaces, amidst fresh air and rural surround ings, so that riding, running, swimming, and all honest personal exercises of offence and defence, together with music and the dance, may be encouraged as primal heads of bodily education. In "Time and Tide" he says:—"The body must be made as beautiful and perfect in its youth as it can be, wholly irrespective of ulterior purpose. If you mean afterwards to set the creature to business which will degrade its body and shorten its life, first, I should say, simply,—you had better let such business alone;—but if you must have it done, somehow, yet let the living creature whom you mean to kill, get the full strength of its body first, and taste the joy, and bear the beauty of youth. After that, poison it, if you will. Economically, the arrangement is a wiser one, for it will take longer in the killing, than if you began with it younger; and you will get an excess of work out of it which will more than pay for its training."

Not only are bodily accomplishments to be *taught*, but mental graces are to be *developed*. These graces, which

Ruskin believes to be innate in every right minded child, are Reverence and Compassion. For the development of reverence three things are essential :—Tuition from masters of high moral tone who will at once secure the love and respect of those whom they teach ; the patient exposition of incidents in historic records which recount the heroic deeds of the world's great men ; and a revelation to the child of the smallness of its own attainments when brought into comparison with those of others. Compassion is to be developed by counting it shameful and cowardly to do a cruel thing, unmanly and criminal to inflict pain on all weak creatures, and in daily disciplining the child to all offices of practical help.

The development of these mental graces is to be followed by an enforcement of five cardinal virtues :—Truthfulness, Justice, Temperance, Bravery, and Obedience. Truthfulness implies accuracy of statement in all principles of honour, and accomplishments of language in daily speech ; the word is to become the bond, and conversation free from exaggeration. Justice consists in granting to every human being due aid in the development of such faculties as it may possess for action and enjoyment—primarily for useful action. Temperance is the power which governs intensest energy, rightly directing its aim, and wisely controlling its force, and getting out of it the greatest amount of usefulness and enjoyment it can possibly yield. Courage is the spirit of fearlessness which responds in spite of all risk ; and Obedience the promptness and steadfastness which fulfils and endures in the manifold duties of life.

Equally pertinent are his suggestions on the cultivation of

the intellectual forces. He recommends that early in life
the child should be grounded in the Greek, Latin, French,
and German languages, not so much with an eye to fluency
of speech or accuracy of translation therein, but in order to
secure them as aids in the mastery of the mother tongue.
"In order to deal with words rightly, this is the habit you
must form. Nearly every word in your language has been
first a word of some other language—of Saxon, German,
French, Latin, or Greek; (not to speak of Eastern and
primitive dialects). And many words have been all these;
—that is to say, have been Greek first, Latin next, French
or German next, and English last: undergoing a certain
change of sense and use on the lips of each nation; but
retaining a deep vital meaning, which all good scholars feel
in employing them, even at this day. If you do not know
the Greek alphabet, learn it; young or old, girl or boy—
whoever you may be, if you think of reading seriously (which,
of course, implies that you have some leisure at command),
learn your Greek alphabet; then get good dictionaries of all
these languages, and whenever you are in doubt about a
word, hunt it down patiently. Read Max Müller's lectures
thoroughly, to begin with ; and, after that, never let a word
escape you that looks suspicious. It is severe work ; but
you will find it, even at first, interesting, and, at last, end-
lessly amusing."

In the study of History he would have the child trained
to work from points of centre, specially selecting for such
the history of those great cities which have been the seat of
their country's life, and more or less factors in the growth of
the world. He names, as the most prominent of such,

London, Paris, Florence, Venice, Rome, and Athens, and the works recommended for their respective study are—for London, Stanley's "Westminster Abbey;" for Florence and Venice, Sismondi's "Italian Republics;" for Rome, Livy, Horace, and Gibbon; for Athens, Herodotus, Thucydides, and her poets.

Along with a study of the history of these cities he recommends a study of their literature, selecting Shakespeare as representative of London, Marmontel of Paris, Dante of Florence, Victor Carpaccio of Venice (unfolding his truth in his paintings), Virgil of Rome, and Plato of Athens. Those who propose to follow out this plan will find many hints as to method and interpretation in the pages of "Fors Clavigera," especially in relation to the study of Dante, Carpaccio, and Marmontel.

The child is also to be trained to study the sciences; not in order to make it a cold and cruel spectator, or a listless observer of the wonders of the universe, but to give it a practical knowledge of surrounding things. In this realm Ruskin's classification is three-fold: Botany, Geology, and Ornithology; the study of such commencing with the district in which the child resides. He is to know the flora of his own neighbourhood, the history of the soil on which he has been reared, as well as the note and habit of every bird that warbles over him its morning song. Ruskin's methods of teaching these sciences will be found in his works entitled "Proserpina," "Deucalion," and "Love's Meinie."

Thus, Ruskin would open out life to the child, and shape the child for life; thus he would cultivate sight and sentiment; while, in order to save from the pride that so often

comes with learning, he would secure as the presiding spirit
and the pervading temper of every life the three-fold influence
of admiration, hope, and love ;—the dispositions which
discern and delight in all that is beautiful in visible form,
and lovely in human temper; which recognise by true
foresight better things to be reached hereafter, and pulse
with tenderness towards all things human, living, and
lovely.

The reader may be prompted to say that such a system of
education is altogether impracticable. So it would be if it
were proposed to apply it indiscriminately to every child.
But this, Ruskin does not for a moment suggest ; indeed, he
is bitterly opposed to any hard and fast curriculum, holding
that no two children are altogether adapted for the selfsame
system of instruction, or for the selfsame end in life. He
tells us that a child's powers are fixed at birth ; and that as
it is vain to seek to make a silk purse out of a sow's ear, so
it is vain to spend your strength and time and money in
striving to get a Turner or a Titian, a Stephenson or a
Livingstone, out of second and third rate mental and moral
stuff. His words are : " Take most pains with the best
material. Many conscientious masters will plead for the
exactly contrary iniquity, and say you should take the most
pains with the dullest boys. But that is not so (only you
must be very careful that you know which are the dull boys ;
for the cleverest look often very like them). Never waste
pains on bad ground; let it remain rough, though properly
looked after and cared for ; it will be of best service so ;
but spare no labour on the good or what has in it capacity
of good. . . . . . of what unspoiled stuff you find to hand,

cut out the best shapes there is room for ; shapes unalterable, if it may be, for ever. ' The best shapes there is room for,' since, according to the conditions around them, men's natures must expand or remain contracted; and yet more distinctly, let me say, ' the best shapes that there is *substance* for,' seeing that we must accept contentedly infinite difference in the original nature and capacity, even at their purest ; which is the first condition of right education to make manifest to all persons—most of all to the persons chiefly concerned. That other men should know their measure, is, indeed, desirable ; but that they should know it themselves, is wholly necessary."

"'By competitive examination of course?' Sternly, no ! but under absolute prohibition of all violent and strained effort — most of all envious or anxious effort — in every exercise of body and mind ; and by enforcing on every scholar's heart, from the first to the last stage of his instruction, the irrevocable ordinance of the third ' Fors Clavigera,' that his mental rank among men is fixed from the hour he was born,—that by no temporary or violent effort can he train, though he may seriously injure the faculties he has ; that by no manner of effort can he increase them ; and that his best happiness is to consist in the admiration of powers by him for ever unattainable, and of arts, and deeds, by him for ever inimitable."

Thus it will be seen the great end of education, according to the system of Ruskin, is the discovery of mental rank and the preparation of the same for its rightful sphere and labour. This rank must be *found*—it cannot be *manufactured*. "You can't manufacture man, any more than you can manufacture gold. You can find him, and refine him : you dig him out as he lies nugget-fashion in the mountain stream; you bring him home; and you make him into current coin, or household plate, but not one grain of him can you originally produce."

A nation's manhood is the gift of heaven; the nation may fail to discover it, or waste it when discovered; but it can no more add one cubit to its stature, or one ounce to its avoirdupois, as far as intrinsic worth is concerned, than it can alter or increase, in nature and in quantity, the veins of mineral wealth beneath its soil. Of all peoples it may be said, "Unto you a son is born; unto you a child is given;" and it is a proof of a people's wisdom when they know, and enthrone, their choicest sons, duly distinguishing the rank of all their other children, and distributing to them according to their several ability. Ruskin's words are as follows :— " You have a certain quantity of a particular sort of intelligence, produced for you annually by providential laws, which you can only make use of by setting it to its proper work, and which any attempt to use otherwise involves the dead loss of so much human energy. Well, then, supposing we wish to employ it, how is it to be best discovered and refined? It is easily enough discovered. To wish to employ it is to discover it. All you need is, a school of trial in every important town, in which those idle farmers' lads whom their masters never can keep out of mischief, and those stupid tailors' 'prentices, who are always stitching the sleeves in wrong way upwards, may have a try at this other trade." Or again :—" It is not, of course, in my power here to enter into details of schemes of education ; and it will be

long before the results of experiments now in progress will
give data for the solution of the most difficult questions con-
nected with the subject, of which the principal one is the
mode in which the chance of advancement in life is to be
extended to all, and yet made compatible with contentment
in the pursuit of lower avocations by those whose abilities do
not qualify them for the higher. But the general principle of
trial schools lies at the root of the matter—of schools, that
is to say, in which the knowledge offered and discipline
enforced shall be all a part of a great assay of the human
soul, and in which the one shall be increased, the other
directed, as the tried heart and brain will best bear, and no
otherwise; and one thing, however, I must say, that in this
trial I believe all emulation to be a false motive, and all
giving of prizes a false means. All that you can depend
upon in a boy, as significant of true power, likely to issue in
good fruit, is his will to work for the work's sake, not his
desire to surpass his schoolfellows; and the aim of the
teaching you give him ought to be to prove to him, and to
strengthen in him, his own separate gift, not to puff him
into swollen rivalry with those who are everlastingly greater
than he: still less ought you to hang ribands and favours
about the neck of the creature, who is the greatest, to make
the rest envy him. Try to make them love him and follow
him, not struggle with him."

Ruskin is equally urgent in his call for sympathy with the
aspirations and advancement of the young. If the work of
the youth is bold and insolent he would repress it with firmness and contempt; if slovenly he would spur, to rouse from
indolence; or if a vain and foolish ambition is leading a lad

to waste himself in striving to become what he can never possibly be, he would chide, at first gently, but if to no purpose, then sternly and unsparingly. But, on the other hand, he would guard all the promising buds of youth from the chill of the world's scorn, from the frost of its unenthusiastic and cynical criticism. If we have praise we are to give it to the deserving young, for the old, if they be great, are beyond it; if we have help we are to bestow it to the inexperienced and weak : to withhold early help is fatal alike to those from whom withheld, and to the parents or community withholding it.

Such, then, is the system of education which Ruskin advocates. Starting with the child from its first speechless years. he would secure for it surroundings that are heavenly, remembering that the influence of parent, of home, and of nature leave their impress for ever on the rapidly crystallizing disposition; and that the measure of what it becomes in this formative period of youth will be the measure of all it can ever hope to achieve in life. He further reminds us that life is meant by God to be a full complement of parts; a body strong and beautiful; a mind open to and stored with the great facts of the world of nature and of the world of man, and a vigorous moral disposition from out which the virtues and graces spring with a natural freshness, and retain an unwithering bloom. And, lastly, he tells us, and repeatedly tells us, that we cannot manufacture, we can only train; that with all our school boards and modern codes we cannot create, we can only take the material as we have it from God, and, discovering its nature, shape it as best we may for its God-appointed work. Is there, after all, anything so impracticable in these simple rules? While, in their entirety, they do not apply to every child, for every child is not fitted to receive the full measure of them, yet no child is excluded; the poorest in station, the feeblest in intellect are considered, and provided for in their general sweep. "I believe *every man in a Christian kingdom ought to be equally well educated.* But I would have his education to purpose; stern, practical, irresistible, in moral habits, in bodily strength and beauty, in all faculties of mind capable of being developed under the circumstances of the individual, and especially in the technical knowledge of his own business; but yet, infinitely various in its effort, directed to make one youth humble, and another confident; to tranquillize this mind, to put some spark of ambition into that; now to urge and now to restrain!"

CHAPTER VII.

ART.

In the third chapter of this book, which contains the
analysis of Ruskin's great works on art and architecture, the
subject of the present chapter is largely foreshadowed ; however, as we are addressing ourselves mainly to the uninitiated,
an amplification of the principles will not be out of place.
Possibility of culture in the field of art is within reach of all :
not that all can be artists, nor all appreciate in the same
measure the manifestations of God in nature, or their
delineations by the hands of men ; but perception of beauty
is possible to all, and power to make some spot beautiful
within reach of all.   A knowledge of the laws of art promotes
the attainment of these ends ; thereby our eyes are opened
to behold the works of Him of whom it is said, "He maketh
everything beautiful in its time," and thereby we are encouraged to make ourselves and our surroundings lovely.
All aid to such culture is worthy our attention ; and if, by
the perusal of this chapter, any reader is led to clearer vision
in beholding the works of nature, or to see a meaning
unseen before in the work of the artist, or if some young
soul is prompted to bring into trial its instinctive powers of
art, and encouraged in the cultivation of lovely things, it will

answer the end for which it is written. It does not profess to be either a systematic or exhaustive arrangement of Ruskin's canons, but simply a collection of some of the broad principles whereby he tests the artist's strength, unfolds the artist's duty, and trains us to perceive the artist's power. We will look, first, at his definition of true art; then treat of the laws to be observed in its cultivation; and lastly, consider its special function—individual and national.

1.—Ruskin's definition of true art.

Perhaps we shall better understand his central idea of true art by showing wherein he distinguishes art from science. In the third volume of "Stones of Venice" this difference is declared to be twofold, namely, in the nature of their actions, and in the nature of the things with which they deal. In action,— science *knows*, art *produces;* in nature of things dealt with,—science treats of things *as they are;* art, with things as they *affect the soul.* The one deals with facts, the other with phenomena; or, to take Ruskin's illustration: "Science informs us that the sun is ninety-five millions of miles distant from, and 111 times broader than, the earth; that we and all the planets revolve round it; and that it revolves on its own axis in 25 days, 14 hours, and 4 minutes. With all this, art has nothing whatever to do. It has no care to know anything of this kind. But the things which it does care to know are these: that in the heavens God has set a tabernacle for the sun, 'which is as a bridegroom coming out of his chamber, and rejoiceth as a strong man to run a race. His going forth is from the end of the heaven, and his circuit unto the ends of it, and there is nothing hid from the heat thereof.'"

8—2

Art, then, sees into the soul of things. Not that it despises the facts made known by science, but, piercing them with instinctive glance, it seizes and declares their spiritual meaning. It not only takes cognizance of "truths of aspect," but its main function is to discover "truths of essence." And hence it is as much vaster in its field than science, "as the soul is larger than the material creation."

This prepares us for Ruskin's further definition :—All great art is revelation ; and all great art is praise.

All great art is revelation. We have just seen that in every object there is a dual nature—an aspect and an essence. In a tree, for example, there are not only the laws of radiation and individuality which appeal to the senses, but behind these lies a law of mystery, of which radiation and individuality are but the outward form. In every mountain range there is not only altitude and outline, but an under-meaning of majesty revealing "the strength of the hills to be His also." In every human countenance there are lines and shades and features distinguishing one man from another, yet these are but the expressions of the *soul*, the inscriptions of the invisible force—the spirit within. Now, true art pierces through all appearances ; it passes by the aspect and secures the essence, of which aspect is the clothing. There are few men who possess this penetrative power. The men who do—the men who see—and who by their representations make others see what they see them-selves, are true artists, and their work true art. All else is mere imitation ; no matter how accurate the line, how true the colour, how vast the scale on which the work is executed, it is mere imitation, cold mechanism, "dead perfection," nothing more. The true artist sees, and makes others see. Note the following extract taken from "Modern Painters":—

"We constantly recognise things by their least important attributes, and by help of very few of these: and if these attributes exist not in the imitation, though there may be thousands of others far higher and more valuable, yet if those be wanting, or imperfectly rendered, by which we are accustomed to recognise the object, we deny the likeness; while, if these be given, though all the great and valuable and important attributes may be wanting, we affirm the likeness. Recognition is no proof of real and intrinsic resemblance. We recognise our books by their bindings, though the true and essential characteristics lie inside. A man is known to his dog by the smell, to his tailor by the coat, to his friend by the smile; each of these knows him, but how little, or how much, depends upon the dignity of the intelligence. That which is truly and indeed characteristic of the man, is known only to God. One portrait of a man may possess exact accuracy of feature, and no atom of expression; it may be, to use the ordinary terms of admiration bestowed on such portraits by those whom they please, 'as like as it can stare.' Everybody, down to his cat, would know this. Another portrait may have neglected or misrepresented the features, but may have given the flash of the eye, and the peculiar radiance of the lip, seen on him only in his hours of highest mental excitement. None but his friends would know this. Another may have given none of his ordinary expressions, but one which he wore in the most excited instant of his life, when all his secret passions and all his highest powers were brought into play at once.

None but those who had then seen him might recognise
this as like. But which would be the most truthful likeness
of the *Man?* The first gives the accident of the body—the
sport of climate, and food, and time—which corruption
inhabits and the worm waiteth for. The second gives the
stamp of the soul upon the flesh; but it is the soul seen in
the emotions which it shares with many; which may not be
characteristic of its essence—the result of habit, and education, and accident—a gloze, whether purposely worn or
unconsciously assumed, perhaps totally contrary to all that is
rooted and real in the mind which it conceals. The third
has caught the trace of all that was most hidden, and most
mighty, when all hypocrisy, and all habit, and all petty and
passing emotion—the ice, and the bank, and the foam
of the immortal river — were shivered and broken, and
swallowed up in the awakening of its inward strength; when
the call and claim of some divine motive had brought into
visible being those latent forces and feelings which the
spirit's own volition could not summon, nor its consciousness comprehend; which God only knew, and God only
could awaken—the depth of the mystery of its peculiar and
separating attributes. And so it is with external Nature:
she has a body and a soul like man; but her soul is the
Deity. It is possible to represent the body without the
spirit; and this shall be like, to those whose senses are only
cognizant of body. It is possible to represent the spirit in
its ordinary and inferior manifestations; and this shall be
like, to those who have not watched for its moments of
power. It is possible to represent the spirit in its secret and
high operations; and this shall be like, only to those to

whose watching they have been revealed. All these are truth; but according to the dignity of the truths he can represent or feel, is the power of the painter, and the justice of the judge."

This power to see and feel is instinctive: it cannot be manufactured. You may train it, or you may destroy it: but make it, or acquire it—never. It is God's gift; a power He dispenses or withholds at His will; a power, the bestowal of which puts a man into possession of the secrets of His nature and the meaning of His works. It is independent of all rules; its mightiest energies manifest themselves without effort; it spends no time in selection or arrangement; its conceptions are instantaneous; it cannot tell you why it did that thing, nor how; it did it because it could not help doing it, and because it could not do it in any other way. "From the bee," says Ruskin, "to Paul Veronese, all master workers work with this awful and inspired unconsciousness."

Further—all great art is praise. It is the expression of the passionate delight of a great soul in the objects it loves most to contemplate. No great painting was ever produced by a passionless hand; the artist must admire ere he can reveal. The habitual attitude of the true artist's mind is reverence, and as you look upon his work you behold the expression of its adoration. "Art is valuable or otherwise, only as it expresses the personality, activity, and living perception of a good and great soul, it may express and contain this with little help from execution, and less from science; and if it have not this, if it show not the vigour, perception, and invention of a mighty human spirit, it is worthless. Worthless, I mean, as *art;* it may be precious in some other way, but, as art, it is nugatory. Once let this be well understood among us, and magnificent consequences will soon follow. Let me repeat it in other terms, so that I may not be misunderstood. All art is great, and good and true, only so far it is distinctively the work of manhood in its entire and highest sense; that is to say, not the work of limbs and fingers, *but of soul.*"*

Or, again :—" As soon as the artist forgets his function of praise in that of imitation, his art is lost. His business is to give, by any means, however imperfect, the idea of a beautiful thing ; not, by any means, however perfect, the realization of an ugly one. In the early and vigorous days of Art, she endeavoured to praise the saints, though she made but awkward figures of them. Gradually becoming able to represent the human body with accuracy, she pleased herself greatly at first in this new power, and for about a century decorated all her buildings with human bodies in different positions. But there was nothing to be praised in persons who had no other virtue than that of possessing bodies and no other means of expression than unexpected manners of crossing their legs. Surprises of this nature necessarily have their limits, and the Arts founded on Anatomy expired when the changes of posture were exhausted."

A great artist, then, is one who sees, and one who feels, and one who is in possession of a power to express his sight and sentiment; he being the greatest whose sight and sentiment take in the loftiest truths, and give to them the

* The italics are ours.

faithfullest portrayal. And he is the best judge of art who has the power to see furthest into the representations of the artist, and who enters most fully into sympathy with the passions therein made manifest.

2.—Laws to be observed in the cultivation of the art faculty.

Though the powers of the artist are a gift, and not an acquirement, such powers are by no means to be neglected; and though, when at full strength, they become impatient of rule, and act independently of it, yet such freedom is never the freedom of license, but of restraint. The men most independent of rules are independent of them only as they submit themselves to other and higher powers: freed from formalism, they are captives to a divine law. Such law they cannot define; all they know is that they are compelled to obey it; it reveals itself to them, and dominates them: they are no longer their own. The uninitiated reader must not suppose that when Ruskin speaks of freedom from rule and exemption from effort as characteristic of the great artist, he implies either carelessness or recklessness; he refers to the freedom of captivity and the repose of strength.

However great the genius, discipline is essential for its right direction and its highest use; undisciplined, it may run to waste, or, what is worse, lay all around it waste in its destructive play. Hence, Ruskin defines an artist as one who has submitted to a law it was painful to obey, that he might bestow a delight it was gracious to bestow. Not that the term "painful" implies an obedience irksome or distasteful in its nature, but an obedience willingly accepted and joyously fulfilled; nevertheless, an *obedience*;—a submission and discipline—or, in other words, a strait gate through which all must pass who are to be kings in the realm of art. No great work is wrought without labour, and though the finely drawn line, and quiet strength discoverable in a painting, may point to consummate ease, yet such ease is purchasable only at the cost of hours of exercise, and days of severest toil ; hence the aphorisms xxi. and xxii. in the " Laws of Fésole " : " When you would do your best, stop the moment you begin to feel difficulty. Your drawing will be the best you can do; but you will not be able to do another so good to-morrow. When you would do *better* than your best, put your full strength out the moment you feel a difficulty. You will spoil your drawing to-day ; but you will do better that your to-day's best to-morrow."

The laws the artist is to learn to obey cover the threefold divisions of outline, colour, and shade. Of these, Ruskin says, outline, in perfection, is the most arduous : nevertheless it is to be the initial step in all art training, and no student is to count himself master of it until he can *see* the end of it, though *reach* that end he never can. Colour, he tells us, is easy, if we can see colour, but impossible if we cannot ; while to shade is exceedingly difficult—only a few masters having reached the perfections of light and shadow. Yet the majority may arrive at such perfection as will enable them to produce good work.

Having attained proficiency in these three divisions, the following laws are laid down as essential in all true art.

(1) " In drawing, try to represent the *appearance* of things, never what you know the thing to be ;" in other words, draw what you *see*, and not what you know.

(2) " Those appearances you are to test by the application of scientific laws relating to aspect; and to learn, by
accurate measurement, and the most fixed attention, to
represent with absolute fidelity;" or, draw what you see *as
you see it*—accurately.

(3) " Having learned to represent actual appearances
faithfully, if you have any human faculty of your own,
visionary appearance will take place to you which will be
nobler and more true than any actual or material appearance; and the *realization* of this is the function of every fine
art, which is founded absolutely, therefore in truth, and
consists absolutely in imagination;" or, treat your facts
imaginatively.

In order to simplify these laws, let us illustrate them
respectively by tracing their fulfilment in a well-known
painting. We shall thus see wherein lies their application
to real work.

Most readers will have seen an engraving, if not the
original painting from the hand of Turner, of a picture
known as "The Fighting Téméraire." The shadows of
evening are deepening, and the sun throws a farewell flood
of glory from the departing day; above, myriads of cloudlets
are aglow with its light, and the crescent moon steals forth
upon her nightly march; beneath, the waters, already
darkening, reflect a sheen as of a pathway of gold, crossed
here and there by the boats of the returning toilers of the
sea. In the foreground is a huge French man-o'-war, with
fractured hull, towed to its last haven by a small steam tug;
the day of its glory for ever departed, it will sail the seas no
more.

Look closely into this picture, and you will see the fulfilment of the three laws now under consideration.

(1) Draw what you *see*,—not what you know. Now, note first, there are ropes left out in the painting which we know are to be found in the vessel; the yards are seemingly unsupported, the masts appear to be without the necessary rigging. How is this? From the distance at which Turner has placed the ship the rigging would be invisible—beyond the range of his eye; he knew it would be there, but he was not painting what he knew would be there, but what he would see there. Likewise, the stern windows and portholes of distant ships are all omitted! Turner knew this, but as he could not have seen them at the point from which he painted, according to the rule paint what you *see*, and not what you *know*, he left them out.

(2) Draw *accurately* what you see. Turn now to the sky and background of the painting, and you will find this second rule faithfully fulfilled. All the cloud-forms are taken from, and are true to, cloud-forms in nature. The rays of light, the shadows cast from the cloudlets, the infinity of grandeur in sky, as well as the ripples on the water, are all accurate representations of these as seen in nature, and not the product of the fancyings of the studio.

(3) Treat your facts *imaginatively*; and in a marvellous manner does Turner in the above instance obey this law. The setting sun images forth the departing glory of the old Téméraire, while the first quarter of the new moon represents the ascendancy of steam power over the old wooden ships, with their sweep of canvas sail, as seen in the tug towing the vessel into port. There seems to be sadness, too,

in the old sun as he takes his last farewell of the fighting ship he has so often companioned on the deep: no more will the dawn cheer the eye of the weary watch, never again will the light gleam on the swelling sails; the sun has aided the captain in his last reckoning, the days of warfare are over, the vessel's work is done.

This function of the imagination, as will be remembered, is threefold:—Associative, or the power to create new forms through combination; penetrative, or the power to appre- hend; and contemplative, or the mode in which the associa- tive and penetrative faculties work. It is the wealth of this imaginative power which gives greatness to the artist, and in proportion to his faculty for displaying it will be his rank as a painter and the worth of his work.

3.—The special function of art.

Has art a noble sphere, or is it but a useless pursuit filling up the hours of the idle, and satisfying the whim of the connoisseur? Ruskin tells us it can only be studied rightly when undertaken for the furtherance of useful ends; and that it can no more be taken up successfully as a pastime than playing at soldiers can train for the field. The true artist submitted to the law that it was painful to obey in order to bestow a delight which it was gracious to bestow. The special function of art is in the bestowment of this delight.

Art is not only a discipline to the artist, but through him it becomes educative and delightful to the individual. The work of a true picture is to get at the imaginative faculty of the beholder, not only quickening, but training it by the representation of truth. Should the imaginative faculty fail to be roused, then there is something wrong either on the part of the spectator or picture; should the picture be demonstrably true, the probabilities are that it is in the spectator; should even the picture be true, unless it arouses the imagination, it fails in its function;—it must first waken and then teach.

But it may be said, Why not cultivate the imagination by bringing it face to face with nature, rather than in second-hand contact with man's copy of nature? We have before stated that no great artist is a copyist; his strength is not in his faultless imitation, but in his expression of the great spirit-truths of nature. Therefore, pictures, if true, and if the production of the seer, unfold nature to us as it never would unfold itself to our unaided sense: they are revelations, and, in the highest sense, educative. To be in possession of a great painting may be likened to being in the company of a great artist as he surveys some stretch of landscape, or looks into the fastnesses of some ravine. How instructive are his descriptions, how wonderful his interpretations, and how inspired his imaginings; how much more we see, how much more we feel, for his companionship! But inasmuch as we cannot have such companionship in person, art enables us to have that of his pictures, wherein he has told us in line and colour all that he would have told us in gesture and word. Ruskin tells us we may say, "To the little and affected painter, 'Stand aside, from between nature and me,' but to the great imaginative painter, greater a million times in every faculty of soul than we, our words may wisely be, 'Come between this nature and me,—this nature which is too great, and too wonderful for me,—interpret it to me—let me see with your eyes, and hear with your ears, and have the help and strength of your great spirit.' "

Art, in its national function, is twofold :—it is related to morals, and it is related to use.

In its relation to morals Ruskin claims for it a power to perfect—not produce—the ethical state of a people ; given, says he, a right moral condition, and it will enchance and complete such condition ; while in its relation to utility it will give delightfulness to the implements of daily use, to materials of dress, to furniture and lodging, and make permanently visible much which otherwise could neither be described by science nor retained by memory.

The ever-recurring refrain of Ruskin's writings for forty years has been : Apply the principles of art to the reformation of national life ; train your sons and daughters to see and to love the beautiful ; cultivate their higher instincts, call forth and feed their souls. Indeed, all his teaching concerning art is a mighty sermon on those Apostolic words : " Finally, brethren, whatsoever things are true, whatsoever things are reverend, whatsoever things are pure, whatsoever things are lovely, whatsoever things are gracious ; if there be any virtue, and if there be any praise, think of these things."

CHAPTER VIII.

POLITICAL ECONOMY.

IT is with considerable reluctance that we approach this
section of Ruskin's works, not so much from uncertainty as
to the soundness of his principles, as from the fact that their
exposition and enforcement invariably arouse misunder-
standing and rancour. Anyone carefully read in his earlier
writings will be prepared, if not expectant, for these last and
crowning conclusions; but to the commercial man, ignorant
of Ruskin as a teacher, and saturated with the ideas of the
modern economic school, they are altogether incompre-
hensible. The attitude of those who form the commercial
circles towards this portion of his teachings has been one
of antagonism. Many who have listened patiently and
appreciatively to him when talking to them about pictures,
flatly refuse to listen to him when he talks about political
economy. The conflict has been long and severe, and harsh
measures have been resorted to on both sides. The torrents
of scorn, and the unsparing impeachment with which
Ruskin has swept down upon what he deems the purblind
selfishness of the moneyed classes, are among the finest passages of invective in the English language; while the savage
and desperate blows aimed in return are proof that those

attacked are not slow in standing on their own defence, nor in fighting for what they suppose to be the national weal. There can be little doubt that the protracted illness from which Ruskin has never fully recovered resulted from wounds received in the fray; while not a few of his opponents will carry to their grave the smart of many of his blows. However, when the battle is for truth the warfare is healthful; and we would not for a moment suppose that either side does not in all sincerity believe in the principles for which it contends. Few even of Ruskin's opponents will question his honesty of purpose in propagating these principles; and few of his followers will refuse to grant honesty of purpose to the leaders of the moneyed and mercantile school. In all controverted questions, where great principles are at stake, it behoves us to understand clearly the positions of either party, and to weigh calmly the statements advanced. It is to this end, and with unshaken faith in an Englishman's innate love of truth and fair-play, that we venture to unfold the views on Political Economy as held by Ruskin, and compare them with those of the modern economic school.

Ruskin defines Political Economy as follows: — "As domestic economy regulates the acts and habits of a household, Political Economy regulates those of a society or State, with reference to the means of its maintenance. Political Economy is neither an art nor a science; but a system of conduct and legislature, founded on the sciences directing the arts, and impossible, except under certain conditions, of moral culture."

" By the maintenance of a State is to be understood the support of its population in healthy and happy life; and the

increase of their numbers, so far as that increase is consistent with their happiness.   It is not the object of Political
Economy to increase the number of a nation at the cost of
common health and comfort; nor to increase indefinitely
the comfort of individuals by the sacrifice of surrounding
lives, or possibilities of life."

Ruskin defines Wealth as consisting of things essentially
valuable; such things, for the sake of convenience, being
referred to the five following :

1. Land, with its associated air, water and organisms.

2. Houses, furniture, instruments.

3. Stored or prepared food, medicine, and articles of
bodily luxury, including clothing.

4. Books.

5. Works of art.

The great law which is to govern the production and
distribution of this wealth is the Law of Co-operation, the
highest and first law of the universe, and the other name of
life—help. This law, Ruskin contrasts with the law of
separation—the other name of death ; his own words being :
"Government and Co-operation are in all things, and
eternally, the laws of life. Anarchy and competition,
eternally, and in all things, the laws of death."

In unfolding the meaning of the term Co-operation, as
used by himself in his own system of Political Economy,
he says : "When I use the word 'Co-operation,' it is not
meant to refer to these new constitutions of firms.   I use the
word in a far wider sense, as opposed, not to masterhood,
but to *competition*.   I do not mean, for instance, by Co-operation, that all the master bakers in a town are to give a share

of their profits to the men who go out with the bread; but that the masters are not to try to undersell each other, nor seek each to get the other's business, but are all to form one society, selling to the public under a common law of severe penalty for unjust dealing, and at an established price. I do not mean that all banker's clerks should be partners in the bank; but I do mean that all bankers should be members of a great national body, answerable as a society for all deposits; and that the private business of speculating with other people's money should take another name than that of 'banking.' And, for final instance, I mean by 'Co-operation' not only fellowship between trading *firms*, but between trading *nations;* so that it shall no more be thought (as it is now, with ludicrous and vain selfishness) an advantage for one nation to undersell another, and take its occupation away from it; but that the primal and eternal law of vital commerce shall be of all men understood—namely, that every nation is fitted by its character, and the nature of its territories, for some particular employment or manufactures; and that it is the true interest of every other nation to encourage it in such speciality, and by no means to interfere with, but in all ways forward and protect, its efforts, ceasing in all rivalship with it, so soon as it is strong enough to occupy its proper place."

This great law of Co-operation is to be brought to bear upon—1st. The *application* of labour, or the obtaining of the most precious and lasting things; not growing oats where you can grow wheat, nor using iron where timber is durable; 2nd. *Preservation*, as the careful storage of wheat and timber from decay; and, 3rd. *Distribution*, as in storage of wheat where it is most needed, and timber within reach at time of call.

Let us now compare these definitions of Ruskin's with those supplied to us by the teachings of the Orthodox School of Economists.

They define wealth as consisting of a stock of useful articles. If we question them as to what they mean by useful articles, they reply: "Things that supply human wants." If we press them further, and ask them what human wants are, they immediately stop us by reminding us that Political Economy, as taught in their school, has nothing whatever to do with the *nature* of human wants—only with their supply. So, logically, their definition of wealth comes to this—"A large stock of any articles for which there is a demand."

The great law which lies at the root of the production and distribution of this wealth is termed by them "the economic motive," which term is but an euphonious way of defining selfishness. Says a member of this school: "Man's teeth show him to be a carnivorous animal. Carnivorous animals take more than their due share of prey; and this instinct must be allowed for in man."

Another of its teachers says: "The desire for distinction which comes with us from the cradle, and never leaves us until we go to the grave, may be pronounced to be the most powerful of human passions. The most obvious source of desire for distinction is the possession of superior wealth. It is the one which excites most the admiration of the bulk of mankind, and the only one which they feel capable of attaining. To seem more rich, or, to use a common expression, to keep up a better appearance, than those within their own sphere of comparison, is, with almost all men who are placed beyond the fear of actual need, the ruling principle of conduct."

In thus comparing the distinctive features of the two systems, we find between them a radical divergence—a dissimilarity not of detail only, but of principle. Ruskin regarding wealth as that which is *essentially* valuable in the sustaining of life ; the Orthodox Economist regarding wealth as comparative and exclusive, and begotten by one at the expense of another. Having compared the definitions, let us look at the practical outcome of the two systems when applied to life.

We have seen that the Orthodox Economist ignores the *nature* of the want ; it is the want in relation to *supply* that he solely considers. Ask him if the want be normal ; or if in its supply the welfare of a people is enhanced. His reply is : " Political Economy is engaged in meeting a demand ; with the moral bearings of such demand it has nothing whatever to do." Thus the utility, or value, of all articles is measured by their profit to the producer—not in their effect upon the consumer ; and a people's want—whatever that may be—and the manufacturer's power to supply the same, are supposed to lie at the root of national prosperity, and form the foundation " element " of the modern economic school.

Now, in the system unfolded by Ruskin, there is a vital distinction drawn between the nature of a " want " and the nature of a "need." Men *want* adulterated gin ; but they *need* pure air, healthy toil, and daily exercise. Women *want* fine feathers torn from the plumage of birds ; but they *need* warm clothing, and becoming ornament. Children *want* tarts and candies; but they *need* wholesome oatmeal and new milk. A nation *wants* one hundred thousand rifles wherewith to mangle the manhood, and lay waste the villages, of a neighbouring nation; but it *needs* good tools, and strong men, that it may conquer and command the natural forces of its own soil. Thus, selfishness and ignorance lie at the root of wants, nature at the root of needs.

Modern Political Economy recognises this distinction, and fixes its attention on the *want*, taking selfishness for economic motive. Thereupon it constructs its system of commercial enterprise, successful in proportion to its ability to meet the demands growing out of a people's wants, whatever those wants may be. A people cry out for cheap liquor, and the merchant who can supply their demand at the lowest possible rate is *supposed* to advance his own interests. A people seek for shoddy cloth, and the manufacturer of adulterated goods grows rich, and becomes a supposedly prosperous man. The fickle fashion of a people fixes itself for the moment upon some fancy fabric as an article of dress, and while the fortunes of a few men who have a royalty on this speciality are secured, the trade of a town like Bradford is brought to ruin. Political economists are logical, and acknowledge selfishness as the "economic motive"; Ruskin is logical, and shows its disastrous workings among the people at large.

But, say the economists, our work is not to educate: it is to supply. Turning upon Ruskin and others, they exclaim, "It is your work to elevate the masses: implant in them higher desires; transform their wants into needs, and we will delight to respond to the supply of their higher demands." (And, be it said, that few merchants of high moral tone delight in supplying that which destroys or, which, in its manufacture, is adulterated ; they would rather put the best of their strength into life-giving articles, and genuine materials ; but, as they say, they are embarked upon the stream, and to resist it would be ruin.) Ruskin accepts the challenge to educate the masses, and right nobly has he striven to do so ; but he thinks that masters, as well as men, are in need of education, and that in no relation of life are they so ignorant as in this. He wonders at the blindness of the economists in their willingness to supply that which is destructive alike to those who labour at its production, and those who participate in its consumption. Not only do they thus frustrate the end of those who, by education, seek to raise the tone of a people's aspirations, but, what is worse, they sever, and wittingly keep apart, the functions of commerce and education. Ruskin insists that commerce is educative ; that not only are the wants of a people confirmed in the production of articles that pander to them, but that this production has a reflex influence upon those engaged in it. Not only does the distiller of adulterated spirit confirm the intemperate habits of a nation, but the men he employs in such adulteration are slowly unmanned in following their work. The master *is* an educative factor ; he may deny it, or seek to hide it, but the fact remains ; and whoever makes the getting of money, on these terms, the end of his labour, is seeking individual enrichment at the cost of national beggary ; he may be a mercantile economist, but a political economist he is not—he is a political impoverisher.

Thus, the orthodox system of economy, according to Ruskin, is short-sighted, nay, one-eyed; it sees only its own interests, and those interests are accumulation; it is the science of how to get rich. It does not measure a nation's prosperity by its manhood, but by its riches. Steady markets, large profits, orders in advance, high rate of wages, —these are the measures of national prosperity. "No," says Ruskin, "you may have all this, and yet be poor; your riches may be corrupted, and your garments moth-eaten; your gold and your silver may be rusted, and their rust be a testimony against you." Deeper than material wealth lies the question of moral sources. He says :—" It is impossible to conclude, of any given mass of acquired wealth, merely by the fact of its existence, whether it signifies good or evil to the nation in the midst of which it exists. Its real value depends on the moral sign attached to it, just as sternly as that of a mathematical quantity depends upon the algebraical sign attached to it. Any given accumulation of commercial wealth may be indicative, on the one hand, of faithful industries, progressive energies, and productive ingenuities; or, on the other, it may be indicative of mortal luxury, merciless tyranny, ruinous chicane. Some treasures are heavy with human tears, as an ill-stored harvest with untimely rain; and some gold is brighter in sunshine than it is in substance. And these are not, observe, merely moral or pathetic attributes of riches, which the seeker of riches may, if he choose, despise; they are literally and sternly, material attributes of riches, depreciating or exalting, incalculably, the monetary signification of the sum in question. One mass of money is the outcome of action which has created—another, of action

which has annihilated—ten times as much in the gathering
of it; such and such strong hands have been paralyzed, as if
they had been numbed by night-shade: so many strong
men's courage broken, so many productive operations hin-
dered; this and the other false direction given to labour,
and lying image of prosperity set up, on Dura plains dug
into seven-times-heated furnaces. That which seems to be
wealth may in verity be only the gilded index of far-reaching
ruin; a wrecker's handful of coin gleaned from the beach to
which he has beguiled an argosy; a camp-follower's bundle
of rags unwrapped from the breasts of goodly soldiers dead;
the purchase-pieces of potter's fields, wherein shall be buried
together the citizen and the stranger."

It will thus be seen that the present system of Political
Economy seeks multiplication of exchangeable articles, while
the system of Political Economy as taught by Ruskin seeks
the multiplication of men. If the highest product of a
nation is its men, if the truest economy aims at the exten-
sion of life, then it is not difficult for us to take sides; even
those most ignorant of social and economic questions will
be able to decide as to which position is most beneficial to
a people, and most permanent to the interests of a State.
Intrinsically considered, there is nothing of higher value to
a nation than her sons. Whatever else she may possess—
stretch of territory, store of treasure, strength of material
power—if in their possession she has sacrificed or neglected
her children she is poor, her birthright is bartered; and
should the hour of her sorrow strike, she will find no place
for repentance though she seek it with tears. We may, as a
nation, point to our world-wide markets, our unwearying

commercial enterprise, and to the fabulous fortunes built up by our so-called self-made men; but these cannot hush the strange whispers, nor lay low the unwelcome spectres, that in quiet hours haunt our hearts. Deep down in the inner consciousness of the nation there is a sense of shame, a felt presentiment that the day of reckoning is at hand. When that day dawns will the nation be enabled to say, pointing to her countless children, "Of them which thou hast given me I have lost none;" or, rather, will she not, beholding their ghastly shapes—manhood crippled by the toil that kills, and womanhood wasted by the selfishness that consumes— cry out in despair, "Am I my brother's keeper?"

The point of divergence is radical; the practical embodiment of Ruskin's system would involve a complete revolution and readjustment in the commercial world. He has put the two positions in the following form:—"I wish the reader clearly and deeply to understand the difference between the two economies, to which the terms 'Political' and 'Mercantile' might not unadvisably be attached. Political Economy (the economy of a State, or of Citizens) consists simply in the production, preservation, and distribution, at fittest time and place, of useful or pleasurable things. The farmer who cuts his hay at the right time; the shipwright who drives his bolts well home in sound wood; the builder who lays good bricks in well-tempered mortar; the housewife who takes care of her furniture in the parlour, and guards against all waste in her kitchen; and the singer who rightly disciplines, and never overstrains her voice: are all political economists in the true or final sense; adding continually to the riches and well-being of the nation to which they belong. But mercantile economy, the economy of 'merces or of pay,' signifies the accumulation, in the hands of individuals, of legal or moral claim upon, or power over, the labour of others; every such claim implying precisely as much poverty and debt on one side, as it implies riches or right on the other."

Ruskin's now almost forgotten controversy with the late Bishop of Manchester, Dr. Fraser, on the question of usury, now claims our notice. It is well known that Ruskin denounces the taking of any instalment, by way of interest, on money lent; and that the only repayment he deems just is that of the principal borrowed. He bases this view upon two broad principles hard to gainsay :—first, that usury, or interest, contradicts the law of brotherhood; second, that eventually it is detrimental to borrower and lender alike.

The very fact that he bases his first position on the law of love, which recognises in every man a brother, puts him out of court with Political Economists. Knowing this, he thus forestalls their objection :—" Ordinary political economists would say,—it is indeed true that certain advantages of a general nature may be obtained by the development of the social affections. But political economists never professed, nor profess, to take advantage of a general nature into consideration. Our science is simply the science of getting rich."

But Ruskin cannot ignore the element of social affection in social action : he cannot overlook the *brother* in the man. Nor can he separate the principles of Biblical teaching from the duties of every-day life. He finds in his Bible what he believes to be a condemnation of usury, and fails to discover

in the laws of Moses, Jesus, and Paul, approval of the line
of action that lends a thousand pounds at five per cent. per
annum, and after the payment of a thousand pounds thereon
for twenty years of interest, demands a thousand more by
way of repayment of principal. We well know that the
majority of men differ widely from Ruskin, not only in their
interpretation of the Bible, but in setting aside the Bible as
a manual for business life; they assent to its inspiration,
but practically contravene it, or, at any rate, make it a
matter of convenience as to the truths they adopt or
abandon. Nevertheless, to mock at Ruskin because his
morals of trade are based primarily upon the Sermon on the
Mount, ill-becomes those who profess to be jealous for the
honour of their Master.

There is, however, the further ground of its inutility as
an educative factor. If life be not educational it is not
worth the living; it becomes a curse, and degeneration its
only law. The value of all life's actions is in their power to
call forth faculties and feelings which widen our usefulness,
intensify our joy, and perfect our manhood. The law of life
is a law of growth, and all that contradicts or frustrates such
law is a factor for death : such destructive forces are started
in the system of loan on interest. When a man lends for
selfish purposes, what effect has the course of action upon
his character? Does it not feed his acquisitiveness; has it
not a tendency to lessen his effort in the field of manly toil,
and prompt him to make out of his fellows a profit he might
have secured from other and nobler sources? And, further,
does it not lead to indolence and inhumanity? is not the
lender led by it eventually to make others work for him,

and to grow harsher in the terms on which he demands the interest for the loan?

These, then, are the moral effects of usury upon the lender. It feeds his love of gain; it paralyzes his skill as a workman by removing the spur to effort; it encourages indolence, and chokes the love and mercy which are the soul of humanity. Ruskin would not, for a moment, say that all men who had money out at interest were greedy, indolent, or heartless,—far from it. What he says is, that the moral effects of usury point to and further the development of these vices; and it would not be difficult to give instances in our own time of men who have, through the effects of this system, become embodiments of the above-named vices.

Take the effects of usury upon the borrower. This is equally as harmful; he gains thereby no permanent advantage; feeling only immediate results, he considers not its after-effects. Let the following words of Mr. Mackmurdo be carefully weighed:—"Its effect upon the borrower is quite as harmful. At first its poisonous nature and widely-harmful effect are not so keenly felt by the workers. They do not so clearly see its workings. 'The operation of capital is regarded by them only in its effect upon their immediate interests—not as its far more terrific power for evil in its appointment of the kind and object of labour.'

"But soon he begins to feel its effect upon himself. For some time he is able to fight against it; but as soon as it has got full swing, and obtains universal use, the borrower must grow poorer and weaker; the lender must get richer and stronger, it being, as we said, a game of certainties against uncertainties : ' it is heads I win, tails you lose.' "

But Ruskin shall be his own exponent. After speaking of the views held on this subject by Plato, Virgil, Dante, Victor Carpaccio and Shakespeare, he says :—" If after knowing these five men's opinions on practical matters (these five, as you will find, being of the same mind), you prefer to hold Mr. J. S. Mill's and Mr. Fawcett's opinion you are welcome.

" Mr. Fawcett has stated that the interest of money consists of three distinct parts : 1. Reward for abstinence. 2. Compensation for the risks of loss. 3. Wages for the labour of superintendence.

" I will reverse this order in examining the statements ; for the only real question is as to the first, and we had better clear the other two away from it.

" 3. Wages for the labour of superintendence.

" By giving the capitalist wages at all, we put him at once into the class of labourers. . . . So far as he is a labourer, of course, like any other, he is to be paid for his work. There is no question but that the partner who superintends any business should be paid for superintendence ; but the question before us is only respecting payment for doing nothing. I have, for instance, at this moment, £15,000 of Bank Stock, and receive £1,200 a year from the bank, but I have never received the slightest intimation from the directors that they wished for my assistance in the superintendence of that establishment. But even in cases where the partners are active, it does not follow that the one who has the most money in the business is either fittest to superintend it, or likely to do so; it is indeed probable that a man who has made money already will know how to make more; and it is necessary to attach some importance to property as the sign of sense; but your business is to choose and pay your superintendent for his sense, and not for his money. Which is exactly what Carlyle has been telling you for some time; and both he and all his disciples entirely approve of interest, if indeed you are prepared to define that term as payment for the exercise of common-sense spent in the service of the person who pays it.

" 2. Compensation for risk.

" Does Mr. Fawcett mean by compensation for risk, protection from it, or reward for running it? Every business involves a certain quantity of risk, which is probably covered by every prudent merchant; but he does not expect to make a profit out of his risks, nor calculate on a percentage on his insurance. If he prefers not to insure, does Professor Fawcett mean that his customers ought to compensate him for his anxiety; and that while the definition of the first part of interest is extra payment for prudence, the definition of the second part is extra payment for *im*prudence? Or does he mean, what is indeed often the fact, that interest for money represents such reward for risk as people may get across the green cloth at Homburg or Monaco? . . . You cannot get anything out of Nature, or from God, by gambling; only out of your neighbour: and to the quantity of interest of money thus gained, you are mathematically to oppose a precisely equal *dis*-interest of somebody else's money.

"These second and third reasons for interest, then, assigned by Professor Fawcett, have evidently nothing whatever to do with the question. What I want to know is, why the Bank of England is paying me £1,200 a year? It certainly does not pay me for superintendence. And so far from receiving my dividend as compensation for risk, I put my money into the bank because I thought it exactly the safest place to put it in. But nobody can be more anxious than I to find it proper that I should have £1,200 a year. Finding two of Mr. Fawcett's reasons fail me utterly, I cling with tenacity to the third, and hope the best from it.

"The third, or first—and now too sorrowfully the last—of the Professor's reasons, is this: that my £1,200 are given me as the 'reward of abstinence.' It strikes me upon this, that if I had not my £15,000 of Bank Stock, I should be a good deal more abstinent than I am, and that nobody would then talk of rewarding me for it. It might be possible to find even cases of very prolonged and painful abstinence, for which no reward has yet been adjudged by less abstinent England. Abstinence may, indeed, have its reward, nevertheless; but not by increase of what we abstain from, unless there be a law of growth for it, unconnected with our abstinence. 'You cannot have your cake and eat it.' Of course not, and if you don't eat it you have your cake; but not a cake and a half. Imagine the complex trial of school-boy minds, if the law of nature about cakes were: that if you ate none of your cake to day, you would have ever so much bigger a cake to-morrow! which is Mr. Fawcett's view of the law of nature about money, and, alas! many a man's beside—it being no law of Nature whatever, but absolutely contrary to all her laws, and not to be enacted by the whole force of united mankind. Not a cake and a quarter to-morrow, dunce, however abstinent you are—only the cake that you have—if the mice don't get at it in the night. Inte-rest, then, is not, it appears, payment for labour ; it is not reward for risk ; it is not reward for abstinence. What is it ? One of two things it is : taxation, or usury !"

To most of us these views are visionary. And why so? Contented with the relative conditions of our lot, we care not to be disturbed in remembering either what we are, or what we might and *ought* to become. We are " dead at heart, and tame in earth's paddock." What shall we eat and what shall we drink, and wherewithal shall we be clothed "—after these things do we seek. Ruskin's system is absolute ; it treats of men, and their relations in life, in the light of Christianity ; and it must stand or fall upon the possibility of brotherhood, and upon the reality of the Spirit of Love

CHAPTER IX.

MORAL INFLUENCES OF RUSKIN'S WRITINGS.

HAVING briefly outlined the life and teachings of John Ruskin, we purpose, in this chapter, to consider some of the moral influences exerted by his writings upon those who have given to them the careful study they demand. Though devoting himself in his earlier works to art criticism, and in his later ones to the discussion of social and economic questions, his authority, as a teacher, is not in any way restricted to their respective spheres. We have already seen that he has written much on many subjects; and such is his comprehensiveness of treatment, whatever the subject in hand, that few can read him without discovering in his writings suggestiveness and inspiration for every sphere of life. The eager and ever-increasing demand for his books, the passionate devotion he arouses in his followers, and the repeated acknowledgments of indebtedness to him on the part of the leading men in all schools of thought and all branches of activity, lead us to search after the secret, and inquire into the nature of the power he exerts.

We are often told his power over the reader lies in his style; and, in some measure, this is true : undoubtedly he is the most fascinating writer of his age. But to single out this as the only, or even the chief, element of his power, is to betray a superficial acquaintance with his teachings, and with the men they have most influenced.   No doubt there are many who turn to his works, not so much for what he has to say, as for the way in which he says it ; and this is a cause of deepest regret to him, and largely accounts for the changed style of his later writings.   He tells us that owing to the necessity laid upon him to write much while he was young, and when he knew but half-truths, there arose a fondness for clothing his ideas in what he thought were fine words.   " People used to call me a good writer then : now they say I cannot write at all, because, for instance, if I think anybody's house is on fire, I only say, ' Sir, your house is on fire.'   Whereas formerly I used to say, ' Sir, the abode in which you probably passed the delightful days of youth, is in a state of inflammation.'   And everybody used to like the effect of the two *p's* in ' probably passed,' and of the two *d's* in ' delightful days.' "

While there may be some truth in this jocular self-criticism, aimed alike at himself and at his readers, yet those who have felt the fascination and inspiration of his earlier writings will neither forget them, nor cease to read them.   They are the outflowing of a young soul, brim-full of admiration, hope, and love.   They pulse with the early life which cometh from the womb of the morning ; they are fresh with the dew of youth.   There is a frankness, an enthusiasm, a passion in them, entrancing the reader, inspiring the student, and moving even the heart of the critic.   In his later writings there is an increase of severity —there is more of the strength which comes from restraint, and of the sadness which is the inheritance of years. Yet this restraint and sadness lend a point and power which we fail to find in the writings of his earlier years.

Both these styles are peculiarly his own. It is true he acknowledges his indebtedness to Hooker and Herbert, whom he made his earlier models; and to Carlyle and Helps, whom he selected as guides in much of his later thinking; nevertheless, all his work bears his own image and superscription. His writings combine the prophetic and poetic elements : in the same sentence the moral and æsthetic side of truth is seized—a stroke of his pen puts before us what we are to *do* and what we are to *love*. It may be said of him as a writer, "strength and beauty are in his right hand :" a clearness patent to all, a conviction irresistible by few, and an attractiveness of setting, which seizes the imagination and wins the heart—these are characteristics which most of his readers must, from time to time, discover.

For example, take the following from "The Crown of Wild Olive," as illustrative of what we mean. Can anything surpass in clearness this definition of work and play? "Now, roughly, not with vain subtlety of definition, but for plain use of the words, play is an exertion of body or mind, made to please ourselves, and with no determined end ; and work is a thing done because it ought to be done, and with a determined end. You play, as you call it, at cricket, for instance. That is as hard work as anything else ; but it amuses you, and it has no result but the amusement. If it were done as an ordered form of exercise, for health's sake, it would become work directly. So, in like manner, whatever we do to please ourselves, and only for the sake of the pleasure, not for an ultimate object, is ' play,' the pleasing thing, not the useful thing."

Or, take an illustration of the convincing method in which he sets truth. Speaking in the same lecture of the English games, horse-racing and sportmanship, he says : " Through horse-racing, you get every form of what the higher classes everywhere call Play ; that is, gambling : and through game-preserving, you get some curious laying out of ground ; that beautiful arrangement of dwelling-house for man and beast, by which we have grouse and black-cock—so many brace to the acre, and men and women—so many brace to the garret." But note the attractiveness with which the truth is set : " I often wonder what the angelic builders and sur-veyors—the angelic builders who build the many mansions up above there ; and the angelic surveyors who measure that four-square city with their measuring reeds—I wonder what they think, or are supposed to think, of the laying out of grounds by this nation, which has set itself, as it seems, literally to accomplish, word for word, or rather fact for fact, in the persons of these poor whom its Master left to repre-sent Him, what that Master said of Himself—that foxes and birds had homes, but He had none."

There is also a delightsome positiveness—a straight-forward, fearless assertiveness—in his style, which at once secures the attention, and wins the respect of thoughtful readers. They soon discover that Ruskin is in earnest, meaning what he says, and saying what he has to say as though he meant his readers to understand him. He never toys with words —he knows too well their preciousness. Nor

does he deal in opinions—when he opines, he tells us, he
is silent.   He speaks forth his knowledge with surety, and
hence in all his writings there is the dogmatic ring of a great
man.   And there is the humility of a great man also.   Even
his knowledge is, at times, at fault ; and when he discovers
this, he readily and openly acknowledges it.   Of late we
have had an instance of this.   Some time ago he passed a
somewhat sweeping assertion, to the effect that no woman
could paint a truly great picture ; but upon seeing afterwards a great picture from the hand of a woman, he tells
us, he rejoiced to find his former conclusions false.   This is
downright frankness, and it is characteristic of all his writing.
The reader feels this, and, as he reads, he loves the writer
who thus treats him to the sincerity of his thinkings, and
also to the acknowledgments of his mistakes.

But Ruskin's style is neither the sole, nor main secret of
his power.   Indeed, those whom he influences most, care
but little for his style in comparison with the truths declared.
No doubt the arrestive method in which he writes draws
many to the reading of his books, but they do not read very
far ere they are conscious of a power other than that of
style ; and if we mean to discover Ruskin's influence we
must set ourselves to the discovery of this power which most
of his readers acknowledge, and which all his readers feel.

In the first place he is an interpreter of nature.   He takes
the visible garment of creation, and after telling its threads
and showing its colours, lifts it aside, and reveals the soul
which breathes within.   Turning to nature's book, he spells
out words new in meaning, and makes known things kept
secret from the vulgar gaze of man.   There are many to

whom the heavens declared no glory and the earth unfolded no poem, until his writings opened their eyes to see and their hearts to feel; many, who never saw the beauty of cloud-form, nor knew the majesty of the hills, nor felt the sweetness of the meadows, until taught by him in "Modern Painters." But since they have sat at his feet no spot in nature is common, no object in nature unclean. Here lies much of his power : he can bring back to us the wonder of childhood ; he is, in this sense, the restorer of paradise ; we feel that, after all, "Earth's crammed with heaven, and every common bush afire with God ;" and that in spite of the indifference begotten by commerce, and the doubt confirmed by science, "the earth *is* the Lord's and the fulness thereof : the world, and they that dwell therein."

The one who can unveil Divine meanings in creation, and invest with significance unobserved though familiar objects, is bound to have a hold upon men. And this is what Ruskin does for us—he is nature's prophet. Listen to him, as he would teach us of cloud-form :—"It is a strange thing how little in general people know about the sky. It is the part of creation in which Nature has done more for the sake of pleasing man, more for the sole and evident purpose of talking to him, and teaching him, than in any other of her works, and it is just the part in which we least attend to her. Every *essential* purpose of the sky might, so far as we know, be answered, if once in three days, or thereabouts, a great, ugly, black rain-cloud were brought up over the blue, and everything well watered, and so all left blue again till next time, with perhaps a film of morning and evening mist for dew. And, instead of this, there is not a moment of any day of our lives, when nature is not producing scene after scene, picture after picture, glory after glory, and working still upon such exquisite and constant principles of the most perfect beauty, and it is quite certain it is all done for us, and intended for our perpetual pleasure. And every man, wherever placed, however far from other sources of interest or of beauty, has this doing for him constantly. The sky is fitted in all its functions for the perpetual comfort and exalting of the heart, for the soothing it and purifying it from its dross and dust. Sometimes gentle, sometimes capricious, sometimes awful, never the same for two moments together; almost human in its passions, almost spiritual in its tenderness, almost divine in its infinity."

Or take his interpretation of the spirit of the rocks. Speaking of the precipice, he says :—" A group of trees changes the colour of its leafage from week to week, and its position from day to day ; it is sometimes languid with heat and sometimes heavy with rain ; the torrent swells or falls in shower or sun ; the best leaves of the foreground may be dined upon by cattle, or trampled by unwelcome investigators of the chosen scene. But the cliff can neither be eaten, nor trampled down ; neither bowed by the shadow, nor withered by the heat : it is always ready for us when we are inclined to labour ; will always wait for us when we would rest ; and, what is best of all, will always talk to us when we are inclined to converse. With its own patient and victorious presence, cleaving daily through cloud after cloud, and reappearing still through the tempest drift, lofty and serene amidst the passing rents of blue, it seems partly to rebuke, and partly to guard, and partly to calm and chasten, the agitations of the feeble human soul that watches it ; and that must be indeed a dark perplexity, or a grievous pain, which will not be in some degree enlightened or relieved by the vision of it, when the evening shadows are blue on its foundation, and the last rays of the sunset resting on the fair height of its golden Fortitude."

If we turn to the meadows, his words are equally suggestive : "Gather a single blade of grass, and examine for a minute, quietly, its narrow sword-shaped strip of fluted green. Nothing, as it seems there, of notable goodness or beauty. A very little strength, and a very little tallness, and a few delicate long lines meeting in a point—not a perfect point neither, but blunt and unfinished, by no means a creditable, or apparently much-cared-for example of nature's workmanship ; made, only to be trodden on to day, and to-morrow to be cast into the oven ; and a little pale and hollow stalk, feeble and flaccid, leading down to the dull brown fibres of roots.   And yet, think of it well, and judge whether of all the gorgeous flowers that beam in summer air, and of all strong and goodly trees—stately palm and pine, strong ash and oak, scented citron and burdened vine—there be any by man so deeply loved, by God so highly graced, as that narrow point of feeble green.   And well does it fulfil its mission.   Consider what we owe merely to the meadow grass, to the covering of the dark ground by that glorious enamel, by the companies of those soft, and countless, and peaceful spears. . . . . All spring and summer is in them— the walks by silent, scented paths—the rests in noonday heats—the joy of herds and flocks—the power of all shepherd life and meditation—the life of sunlight upon the

world, falling in emerald streaks, and falling in soft blue
shadows, where else it would have struck upon the dark
mould, or scorching dust."

Or, again, take the following description of a stone :—" A
stone, when it is examined, will be found a mountain in minia-
ture.   The fineness of Nature's work is so great, that, into a
single block, a foot or two in diameter, she can compress as
many changes of form and structure, on a small scale, as she
needs for her mountains on a large one ; and, taking moss
for forests, and grains of crystal for crags, the surface of a
stone, in by far the plurality of instances, is more interesting
than the surface of an ordinary hill ; more fantastic in form,
and incomparably richer in colour."

Who can read works, from which the above extracts are
taken, and of which they are not exceptional, but general
examples, without having a clearer vision and warmer heart
for those great works of which it is said, " In wisdom hath
He made them all ?"

Ruskin also possesses the power, peculiar to the few great
of every age, of so putting his soul into his writings that
through them he gets at the souls of his readers.   Of his
words it may be said they are spirit, and they are life.   They
are correctives to indolence, and sources of renewal to those
engaged in noble enterprise ; they come as impulses ; not
stimulants which intoxicate, but nutriment, feeding resolve,
and giving staying power to life.   However feeble a man
may be, they bid him remember he is called for, and capable
of, work ; however lowly his lot, they teach him how he may
find happiness therein : they make the son of toil conscious
of the dignity of labour, and convince the disappointed and

hopeless that no good thing is ever done in vain; the thoughtful find in them truths opening out fields of suggestiveness, and the weary may turn to them for restoration of strength.   We well remember towards the close of a day of disappointment and gloom—a day in which life seemed crowded with mockeries and failure—reading, for the first time, the following words :—"Life is real—not evanescent nor slight.   It does not vanish away; every noble life leaves the fibre of it, for ever, in the work of the world; by so much, evermore, the strength of the human race has gained." Many a time since then we have quoted this passage to down-hearted men, and many a time in life's dark hours repeated it to ourselves, and its strength has been sure.   There are some teachers who interest us, others who dispirit us, but Ruskin's words bring life; and whenever we are engaged at our life-appointed work we know of few, if any, more helpful and inspiriting.   True, he discourages all futile and unnatural effort, and shows scant sympathy with those dissatisfied with their rank, or eager to emulate that which they can never become.   But for those prepared to work with all their might at their God-appointed task, there, where they are, and whatever it may be, the writings of John Ruskin will aid mightily in establishing the work of the hands.

The moral influence of Ruskin is also felt in the direction of social reforms.   Organizations for the improvement of the people have not only been suggested and elaborated in his writings, but, in some cases, started and sustained largely by their motive power.   Many of the picture-galleries, art schools, museums, and working men's clubs, while not directly tracing their origin to his writings, would certainly not have been in existence but for their help. And there are not a few men and women, engaged in philanthropic labour at the present day, who acknowledge his teaching as the force first rousing their efforts, and since guiding and encouraging them in their self-appointed duties among the poor.

His writings are also characterized by spirituality of tone. They are free from the materializing influences common to so much of the teaching of the present age ; their tendency is to purify and ennoble, to enthrone duty, reveal goodness and encourage "admiration, hope, and love." He seeks to rescue man from the engrossing spirit of greed, and woman from the life of frivolity and fashion. He has a profound reverence for the God of his fathers, and firmly holds a belief in the unseen. Righteousness with him is no slowly-evolved quality, but a Divine principle, eternal and unchangeable ; and right and wrong no relative conditions, but absolute, and for ever fixed. Indeed, he has said that if we ask ourselves why we are to do the right, and leave undone the wrong, we disgrace ourselves in the asking. He hates utilitarianism in morals, and warns men that did they even perish like the brutes this would be no excuse for fleshly lives. In what sermon have you more powerful or spiritual teaching than the following : — "Mighty of heart, mighty of mind — 'magnanimous'—to be this, is indeed to be great in life ; to become this increasingly, is, indeed, to 'advance in life,'— in life itself—not in the trappings of it. My friends, do you remember that old Scythian custom, when the head of a house died ? How he was dressed in his finest dress, and set in his chariot, and carried about to his friends' houses; and each of them placed him at his table's head, and all feasted in his presence! Suppose it were offered to you in plain words, as it *is* offered to you in dire facts, that you should gain this Scythian honour, gradually, while you yet thought yourself alive. Suppose the offer were this: You shall die slowly; your blood shall daily grow cold; your flesh petrify; your heart beat at last only as a rusted group of iron valves. Your life shall fade from you, and sink through the earth into the ice of caina; but, day by day, your body shall be dressed more gaily, and set in higher chariots, and have more orders on its breast—crowns on its head, if you will. Men shall bow before it, stare and shout round it, crowd after it up and down the streets; build palaces for it, feast with it at their tables' heads all the night long; your soul shall stay enough within it to know what they do, and feel the weight of the golden dress on its shoulders, and the furrow of the crown-edge on the skull;— no more. Would you take the offer, verbally made by the death-angel? Would the meanest amongst us take it, think you? Yet practically and verily we grasp at it, every one of us, in a measure; many of us grasp at it in its fulness of horror. Every man accepts it who desires to advance in life without knowing what life is; who means only that he is to get more horses, and more footmen, and more fortune, and more public honour, and—*not* more personal soul. He only is advancing in life, whose heart is getting softer, whose blood warmer, whose brain quicker, whose spirit is entering into Living peace."

Is there not a depth of spirituality in that teaching? To

the ughtful readers it is everything when an author can give increased spirituality of tone to life. The world's levels are so low, and manhood so weighted down, that it needs a well-nigh superhuman effort on our part to see the stars. John Henry Newman has said, "The world forgets that men have souls." This is too often true of the world's teachers. They tickle and tease, and delight to tell us we are only dust, or that dust is the only thing worth living for. But if there be a supreme truth flowing out of Ruskin's writings, it is the ennobling and spiritualizing truth that reminds us we were born in the Divine image for Divine ends.

And lastly, Ruskin throws a flood of light upon the Scriptures. Though making no claim to Biblical exegesis, many of his passing comments are marked by critical acumen and expository genius. His interpretation of Psalm xix. in the fifth volume of "Modern Painters;" his lucid passages on "Thy kingdom come," and "Except ye be converted and become as little children," in "The Crown of Wild Olive;" together with his discourses on the adoration of the Shepherds and of the Magi before the Child-King at Bethlehem, in "Fors Clavigera," are examples of what may be found in all parts of his works. His power to make a verse of Scripture interpret a phenomenon in nature, his apt method of reducing prophetic and apostolic principles to every-day life, and his unrivalled skill of interweaving sacred phraseology with his own, make his writings suggestive and interpretative of the greatest of all books. Indeed, it may be said, Ruskin writes as much for preachers as for artists, and we question whether he has not, in spite of cleric scorn, had as powerful an influence over the pulpit as over the

studio.   We are not asserting too much when we say that in
" Modern Painters " there is more religion—both natural and
revealed—than can be found in many a compendium of
theology enforced upon the student of divinity in his college
days ; while the " Seven Lamps of Architecture " and the
" Stones of Venice " contain as searching analyses of the
human heart as any work on Moral Science.   Viewed as a
religious teacher, he may be said to possess more of the
Hebrew Prophet than of the Galilean Apostle ; and he has
proved himself to be as deep a seer into the Divine Word
as he is a true interpreter of the Divine Works.

Take the following as showing his power of insight into
New Testament narrative : " They had gone back to their
daily work, thinking still their business lay netwards—un-
meshed from the literal rope and drag.   Simon Peter saith
unto them, ' I go a-fishing.'   They say unto him, ' We also
go with thee.   True words enough, and having far echo
beyond the Galilean hills.   That night they caught nothing ;
but when the morning came, in the clear light of it, behold,
a figure stood on the shore.   They were not thinking of
anything but their fruitless hauls.   They had no guess who
it was.   It asked them simply if they had caught anything.
They said no.   And it tells them to cast yet again.   And
John shades his eyes from the morning sun with his hand,
to look who it is ; and though the glinting of the sea, too,
dazzles him, he makes out who it is, at last ; and poor
Simon, not to be outrun this time, tightens his fisher's coat
about him, and dashes in over his nets.   One would have
liked to see him swim those hundred yards, and stagger to
the beach.

" Well, the others get to the beach, too, in time, in such slow way as men in general do get in this world to its true shore, much impeded by that wonderful ' dragging the nets with fishes ;' but they get there—seven of them in all—first, the Denier, and then the slowest believer, and then the quickest believer, and then the two throne-seekers, and two more, we know not who."

Or take an instance or two of Ruskin's apt method of turning incidents from the Scriptures into deep and world-wide principles :

"'The sin of the whole world is essentially the sin of Judas. Men do not disbelieve their Christ, but they sell Him."

And again : "'They have no wine.' 'Whatsoever He saith unto you, do it.' The first sentence of these two contains the appeal of the workman's wife to her Son, for the help of the poor of all the earth. The second, the command of the Lord's mother to the people of all the earth, that they should serve the Lord."

Now and again, in a sentence, he opens out the spirit of some oft-repeated and little understood verse of Scripture, as when he says : " You know that to give alms is nothing unless you give thought also ; and that, therefore, it is written, not ' blessed is he that *feedeth* the poor,' but ' blessed is he that *considereth* the poor.' "

As an example of his power of exposition we offer the following, which, though somewhat lengthy, is so clear and so exhaustive, and so little known, that it is worthy of notice :

"'The address to each (the seven churches, Rev. ii., iii.) consists of four parts.

"First. The assertion of some special attribute of the Lord of the Churches, in virtue of which and respect to which He specially addresses that particular body of believers.

"Second. The laying bare of the Churches' heart, as known to its Lord.

"Third. The judgment on that state of the heart, and promise or threat of a future reward or punishment, assigned accordingly, in virtue of the Lord's special attribute, before alleged.

"Fourth. The promise, also in virtue of such special attribute, to all Christians who overcome, as their Lord overcame, in the temptation with which the Church under judgment is contending.

"That we may better understand this scheme and its sequence, let us take first the four divisions of the charge to the Churches :

I. Ephesus.

The Attribute.—That holdeth the seven stars, and walketh in the midst of the seven golden candlesticks.

The Declaration.—Thou hast left thy first love.

The Judgment.—I will move the candlestick out of its place, except thou repent.

The Promise.—(Always 'to him that overcometh') I will give to eat of the tree of life.

II. Smyrna.

The Attribute.—The First and the Last, which was dead and is alive.

The Declaration.—I know thy sorrow and thy patience.

The Judgment.—Be thou faithful unto death, and I will give thee a crown of life.

The Promise.—He shall not be hurt of the second death.

III. Pergamos.

The Attribute.—He which hath the sharp sword with two edges.

The Declaration.—Thou hast there them that hold the doctrine of Balaam.

The Judgment.—I will fight against thee with the sword of My mouth.

The Promise.—I will give him to eat of the hidden manna.

IV Thyatira.

The Attribute.—That hath his eyes like a flame of fire.

The Declaration. — Thou sufferest that woman Jezebel.

The Judgment.—I will kill her children with death.

The Promise.—I will give him the morning star.

V. Sardis.

The Attribute.—That hath the seven spirits of God.

The Declaration.—Thou hast a few names—even in Sardis.

The Judgment.—They shall walk with Me in white, for they are worthy.

The Promise.—I will confess his name before My Father and His angels.

VI. Philadelphia.

The Attribute.—He that hath the key of David.

The Declaration.—I have set before thee an open door.

The Judgment.—I will keep thee from the hour of temptation.

The Promise.—He shall go out of My temple no more.

VII. Laodicea.

The Attribute.—The Beginning of the Creation of God.

The Declaration.—Thou art poor and miserable.

The Judgment.—Behold, I stand at the door and knock.

The Promise.—I will grant him to sit with Me on My throne."

That exposition is indicative of spiritual insight, and a remarkable power of clear and forceful arrangement. We do not wonder that many of his readers are indebted to him not only for his interpretation of the works, but also of the Word of God.

CHAPTER X.

THOUGH few great writers have been more severely criticised, and, in one phase of teaching, uncompromisingly denounced, than John Ruskin, there are not many, even among his less enthusiastic admirers, who deny him front rank among the writers and teachers of his day, or who fear to prophesy for him a prominent position in the near and distant future. There are two ways in which a man projects and perpetuates himself: in other words, his immortality may be monumental or reproductive. If the former, he lives in his works; if the latter, he lives in his words. It is no exaggeration to assert that Ruskin will live in both. His style alone secures him an enduring fame. His books, as models of composition, are bound to be conterminous with the life of the English language. His standards of art criticism have already revolutionized the schools of taste, and will of necessity continue to be factors therein for all time. And whatever the so-called vagaries of his later writings may be, their comprehensiveness, thoroughness, and originality demand a careful study from those who, in any way, profess an interest in the solution of the coming economic and social problems. Ruskin has interwoven himself by his master-style into the future of the nation's literature, and he has interwoven himself by his reformative principles into the future amelioration of the nation's life.

There are three things that give immortality to style—truthfulness, individuality, and life. By truthfulness we mean the selection—the unerring selection—of the best words—the words that most faithfully express the meaning of the writer's thought. Even amongst the noblest words there are degrees, and he is the purest and choicest writer who selects the superlative—the word that says more than any other word because of its succinctness, comprehensiveness, and force. Few writers trouble themselves with this word-truthfulness: they care more for word-melody and word-show. The master of style, however, stakes all upon word-veracity. He selects none with questionable or partial meanings. His aim is to lay hold of those that most faithfully discover to others the inner workings of his mind. Individuality betrays the writer's inherent strength; it at once shows whether he be a mere echo or a voice, a retailer or an originator. Every truly great man has his own style ; for, after all, what is style but the mind's attempt to reveal itself? Just as truthfulness of style bespeaks culture, individuality of style bespeaks strength. Weak men are weak writers ; and no matter how accurate or how beautiful a style may be, if the strong man fails to declare himself the germ of longevity is wanting. Life is the soul that not only gives movement to the style, but imparts movement to the reader. A living style is charged with winged words—words so winged that he who reads is borne along upon their pinions. Movement, energy, inspiration, co-mingling, and imparting themselves to the reader's mind, are the secrets of life—the secrets that make a book a living thing. Now, these three properties may exist separately, and do in many styles. We meet with accuracy without individuality, and with individuality without life. When, however, they are found together, we have the qualities of the highest and most enduring style.

These qualities are the chief characteristics of Ruskin's writing, and will secure for him a posthumous fame. That his style has many minor qualities we admit. Rhythm, imagery, versatility, and other features add to its charm. But not by these will it live; indeed, these will live only because they are the appendages and minor attributes of the great qualities already named.

Ruskin will influence art in the future as he has done in the past; men of all schools will consult him and acknowledge his dicta, whether they are in agreement with them or not. The man who in so short a time could revolutionize those old canons that measured the excellency of a painting by its correspondence with the old masters, and set forth truthfulness to nature as the primal test of value in all art productions, and who even criticised the old masters themselves, showing their deficiencies in their deflections from the works of the Great Parent, cannot possibly part with his influence at his own expiration, or the expiration of his age. Such a school of criticism as his must, in the very nature of things, perpetuate itself, and correct and regulate the art criticism of the future. His fame, too, as an interpreter of art, as well as a critic, is secure. As the study of art becomes more popular, his works will be more in demand. It is not for us here to question whether his interpretations are always exact ; enough for us to know they are always suggestive and inexhaustible ; and suggestiveness and inexhaustibility are sure of welcome and appreciation in time to come. Ruskin has, in many instances, made himself co-temporary with the fame of those whose works he has interpreted. As long as Turner lives Ruskin will live also ; and while men delight to contemplate the beauties and glories of Titian, Raphael, and others of the school of old masters, the writings contributed by Ruskin for the better comprehension of their works will assure for him a rank and claim. Ideas may change, and schools may be revolutionized ; but the interpreter of genius lives because of the life he interprets. This secures for Ruskin a future, and gives him an influence other, and farther reaching, than that of his own age.

It would be folly to defend all Ruskin has said on the great questions of Political Economy and social reform. Mistakes, however, have been made by those who so severely censure him, inasmuch as they forget that the work of reformation is destructive before it can be constructive, and that the two are distinct in nature as well as in order. A man may pull down too rapidly, or he may pull down too much. But he must not be measured merely by what he removes, or by the way in which he removes it. Thoughtful men take into consideration what the reformer offers by way of replacement—that which he gives as well as that which he *takes away* weighs with them in the estimates they form and the judgments they pass. If Ruskin were oftener judged in this twofold light, rather than in the sole light of one who over-

turns and removes, fairer and truer estimates would be given
upon that phase of his teaching which has brought him into
so much disfavour.   The future has claims upon the present
—to-morrow is the child of to-day; and no thoughtful and
unselfish man can shut his eye to these facts, or allow his
life to be uninfluenced by them.   Now, the latter half of
Ruskin's life has been lived beneath the realization of this
important truth.   His teaching has shot ahead of the needs
of his age—that is, the needs as understood and estimated by
selfish men.   It has taken into account the fact that that
which is to be may be all the better by awakening and re-
addressing *that which is*.   He has laid his finger upon social
sores, and irritated them; and unfolded laws of national
health, strict and disciplinary, and enforced them with relentless persistence.   So thorough is his exposure, and so
uncompromising and far-reaching his remedies, that all
those who lay themselves out for the future welfare of the
race can do no other than consult him and more or less be
influenced by him.   Truths, and especially truths in certain
form, and dealing with certain questions, are germinal.   The
all-absorbing question of the immediate future is the
amelioration of the suffering brought about by the rapidly-
earned wealth of the last seventy years.   In our own country
there is a terrible congestion, a congestion which the tinkering of Parliament and the imbecile efforts of well-meaning
philanthropists have only aggravated.   To the removal of
this congestion, the minds of many of our best men are now
turned; and the tide of thought, and the energy of action
setting in this direction, prophesy for the movement an
immediate and all-absorbing prominence.   If this be so,

whatever Ruskin's vagaries and mistakes, his latter works will be the text-books to which the social reformers will turn, and his great remedial schemes, if not models, will be the suggestive lines along which such reformers will work, for they will build from his foundations if they do not pattern after his plans. In this great domain Ruskin will hold his own, and secure his future.

That Ruskin has had, and still has, greater co-temporaries we do not deny; nevertheless, if we limit him to his own order it will be difficult to find his compeer. As writer, reformer, and interpreter his name will for ever claim rank with those whom time is slow to forget and fame discard. His rhythmic sentences discover the tenderest tones, as well as the mightiest power, of our mother tongue; and his far-reaching principles supply the foundation of a national purity and a universal commonweal; while his keen insight into beauty, and his subtle interpretation of the finer issues of artist and poet, place him as one of those expositors without whose aid the careful student cares not to formulate his conclusions. He may not be original in the sense in which highest genius is original; yet he possesses the originality that is in touch with, and reveals, the originality of that higher order. He may not be a leader whom we can always follow, but he will instruct us, and his thoughts will be ever fresh. His may not be the unerring line along which we may always safely travel, but his is always the inspiring breath giving strength to tread wherever duties' path may lead. The man may perish in his system; nay, his system may perish, or rather be absorbed, in systems later born—systems broader and deeper than his own—in part outcomes

of his system, as the blossom is the outcome of the seed.
All this is possible. Yet for long years his position in the
front rank of English writers and teachers is secure.

Ruskin has staked the future of his system upon the truthfulness or otherwise of the three following positions :—
whether there be One true and living God, or no God at
all; whether the old English faith be true or false; and
whether the voice of his own deepest soul has been the
voice of truth, or a mere imagination and a lie. Sure
foundations these, and noble tests. Fearless indeed, as
well as sincere, must he be who submits all he has said and
written to these touchstones; and fearless must we be of
any system rising from such foundations, and staking its all
upon correspondence and truthfulness to the same.

INDEX.

THE END.

BILLING AND SONS, PRINTERS, GUILDFORD.

FREDERICK WARNE & CO.'S
NEW BOOKS.

THE WORKS OF WILLIAM SHAKSPEARE. The "Bedford" Edition.

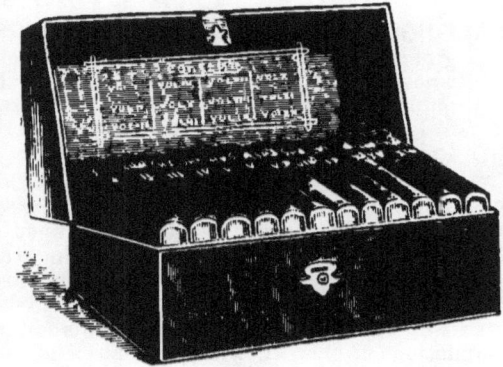

This charming Edition of "Shakspeare's Works" is the only Red-Line Pocket Edition yet issued, and it contains the whole of the Plays and Poems of the great Dramatist, as well as a Memoir and a Glossary.

The Volumes are of the handiest possible size, each measuring $3\frac{1}{2}$ by 5 inches, and they are exquisitely printed on fine paper from New Type specially chosen for its clearness.

Sketch showing paste grain style, with round corners, in new box case.

The Text has been most carefully prepared from comparisons of the best editions, including the celebrated First Folio of 1623 and the Quartos.

It is issued in the following styles :—

In cloth gilt, in neat cloth box, price £1 1s.

And is also kept at prices from One Guinea and a Half upwards:—

In French morocco limp, in neat French morocco case.

In Cabinet style, cloth gilt, gilt top, in handsome polished walnut Cabinet, glass front.

In French morocco limp, in neat French morocco lock case.

In Paste grain, round corners, red under gold edges, in new box case.

In Persian morocco limp, red under gold edges, neat Persian morocco case.

In Turkey morocco limp, round corners, red under gold edges, in elegant Turkey morocco lock case, satin lined.

In Russia limp, round corners, in elegant Turkey morocco lock case, satin lined.

Price £1 1s. per set.

HISTORY OF THE WAR IN THE PENINSULA, and in the South of France, from the Year 1807 to the Year 1814. By Major-General Sir W. F. P. NAPIER, K.C.B. In Six Volumes, with valuable Notes and Fifty-five Maps and Plans. Large crown 8vo, uncut, cloth gilt.

"The value of General Napier's important work on the campaign in the Peninsula is too well known to need further commendation. The edition before us with all its maps and plans is well produced and worthy of a place in every gentleman's library."—*Standard.*

Price £1 per set.

HALF-HOURS WITH THE BEST AUTHORS. Re-modelled by its Original Editor, CHARLES KNIGHT, with Selections from Authors added whose Works have placed them amongst the "Best Authors" since the publication of the First Edition. (Library Edition.) In Four Vols., fully Illustrated with Wood Engravings, Steel Portraits and Complete Index. Crown 8vo, cloth gilt.

This book contains 320 Extracts of the best efforts of our great Standard Authors, whether they be Poets or Historians, Essayists or Divines, Travellers or Philosophers, arranged so as to form half an hour's reading for every day of the year. The student finds a taste of every quality, and a specimen of every style. Should he grow weary of one author, he can turn to another ; and if inclined to be critical, he can weigh the merits of one writer against those of his fellow. Such books are the true foundations of that knowledge which renders men celebrated and famous.

HALF-HOURS OF ENGLISH HISTORY. (Library Edition.) In Four Volumes, with Steel Portraits. Crown 8vo, cloth gilt.

Volumes I. and II., from the Roman Period to the Death of Elizabeth, Selected and Edited, with Notes, by CHARLES KNIGHT.

Volumes III. and IV., containing the History from James to Victoria, by L. VALENTINE.

The work contains the Choicest Historical Extracts from upwards of Fifty Standard Authors, with a General Index.

The articles are chiefly selected so as to afford a succession of graphic parts of English History, chronologically arranged, from the consideration that the portions of history upon which general readers delight to dwell are those which tell some story which is complete in itself, or furnish some illustration which has a separate as well as a general interest.

Price 18s. per set.

THE ABBEYS, CASTLES AND ANCIENT HALLS OF ENGLAND AND WALES: Their Legendary Lore and Popular History. Compiled and Edited by JOHN TIMBS and ALEXANDER GUNN. In Three Vols., with Twelve fine Photographs by FRITH. Vol. I., South ; Vol. II., Midland ; Vol. III., North. Large crown 8vo, cloth gilt, gilt top, bevelled boards.

"This set contains a great deal of curious and valuable information; a description is given of the most striking places of interest in each county, with such details of historical and legendary matter as tend to give additional interest."

THE CHANDOS CLASSICS.

A SERIES OF OVER 130 VOLUMES OF STANDARD WORKS IN POETRY, HISTORY, BIOGRAPHY AND GENERAL LITERATURE.

The Chandos Classics form a complete and well-selected Library, containing the collected wisdom, wit, imagination, and knowledge of all ages and all countries. Since the Publishers first commenced the issue of this large and ever-increasing Collection, their aim has always been to produce the Standard Works of all Nations having a literature, translated by the best English Authors, as well as all the gems and treasures of English Prose and Poetry.

The whole of the Volumes in this Series have been reprinted from the best Editions, and Edited carefully, wherever editorial work was required.

Among them will be found various Volumes of Poetical Works, which are prefixed by brief Memoirs, and have copious Notes and Glossaries, and are fairly entitled to be called the most complete Editions obtainable.

The Volumes are well printed on good paper and tastefully bound.

Published in Four Distinct Styles as follows :

1st. *In neat paper cover, price* **1s. 6d.**

2nd. *Cloth gilt, cut edges, price* **2s.**

3rd. *Library style, smooth dark blue cloth, white label, uncut, price* **2s.**

4th. *Library style extra (imitation Roxburghe), leather label, gilt top, trimmed edges, price* **2s. 6d.**

*** Volumes marked † cannot be supplied in **1s. 6d.** style.

1 **Shakspeare's Complete Works.** The Plays, Poems and Sonnets, together with Memoir and Glossary.

2 **Longfellow's (Henry W.) Poetical Works,** including Recent Poems.

3 **Byron's (Lord) Poetical Works.**

4 **Scott's (Sir Walter) Poetical Works.**

5 **Arabian Nights' (The) Entertainments.** Edited by the Rev. GEORGE FYLER TOWNSEND.

6 **Eliza Cook's Poetical Works.**

7 **The Legendary Ballads of England and Scotland.**

8 **Burns' (Robert) Poetical Works.**

9 **Johnson's Lives of the Poets.** With Critical Observations on their Works, &c., and Sketch of the Author's Life by Sir W. SCOTT.

10 **Dante (The Vision of). Hell** Purgatory and Paradise. CARY's Translation.

11 **Moore's (Thomas) Poetical Works.**

12 **Dr. Syntax's Three Tours.** With Coloured Illustrations.

13 **Butler's Hudibras.** With Notes and Preface by ZACHARY GREY, LL.D.

14 **Cowper's (William) Poetical Works.**

15 **Milton's (John) Poetical Works.**

16 **Wordsworth's (William) Poetical Works.**

17 **Hawthorne's Twice Told Tales.**

18 **England : Its Constitutional History.** Edward I. to Henry VII., by HENRY HALLAM; and The Constitution of England by J. L. DE LOLME.

THE CHANDOS CLASSICS—*continued.*

19 **History of the Saracens,** and the Rise and Fall of their Empire. By EDWARD GIBBON and SIMON OCKLEY.

20 **Lockhart's Spanish Ballads** and|Southey's Chronicle of the Cid.

21 **Robinson Crusoe** (The Life and Adventures of). By DANIEL DEFOE. Now First Correctly Reprinted from the Original Edition of 1719, with an Introduction by WM. LEE, Esq. Illustrations by ERNEST GRISET.

22 **The Swiss Family Robinson.** A New Translation. By Mrs. H. B. PAULL. Fully Illustrated.

23 **Mrs. Hemans' Poetical** Works.

24 **Grimm's Fairy Tales.** Translated by Mrs. H. B. PAULL.

25 **Andersen's (Hans) Fairy** Tales. Translated by Mrs. H. B. PAULL.

26 **Scott's Lives of Eminent** Novelists and Dramatists. By Sir WALTER SCOTT.

27 **Scott's Essays on Chivalry,** Romance and the Drama. By Sir WALTER SCOTT.

28 **Shelley's (Percy Bysshe)** Poetical Works.

29 **Campbell's (Thomas) Poeti-** cal Works.

30 **Keats' (John) Poetical** Works.

31 **Coleridge's (Samuel) Poeti-** cal Works.

32 **Pope's Iliad of Homer.** With Notes by Rev. T. A. BUCKLEY, M.A., F.S.A. Illustrated with Flaxman's Designs.

33 **Pope's Odyssey of Homer.** With Notes by Rev. T. A. BUCKLEY, M.A., F.S.A. Illustrated with Flaxman's Designs.

34 **Hood's (Thomas) Poetical** Works. Complete.

35 **Representative Actors.** A Collection of Criticisms, Anecdotes, Personal Descriptions, &c. &c., from the Sixteenth to the Present Century. With Notes and Memoirs. By W. CLARK RUSSELL.

36 **Romance of History—Eng-** land. HENRY NEALE.

37 **Romance of History —** France. LEITCH RITCHIE.

38 **Romance of History —** Italy. C. MACFARLANE.

39 **Romance of History —** Spain. DON T. DE TRUEBA.

40 **Romance of History —** India. Rev. H. CAUNTER. (Romantic Tales founded on Historical Facts in the History of these Countries.)

41 **German Literature** (Beauties of.) As Exemplified by the Works of PICHLER, RICHTER, ZSCHOKKE and TIERCK. With Biographical Notices.

42 **Don Quixote de la Mancha** (Adventures of). Translated from the Spanish by MOTTEUX.

43 **Eastern Tales.** By many Story-tellers. Compiled and Edited from Ancient and Modern Authors. By Mrs. VALENTINE.

44 **The Book of Authors.** A Collection of Criticisms, ana, mots, Personal Descriptions, &c., referring to English men of Literature in every Age. By W. CLARK RUSSELL.

45 **Pope's (Alexander) Poetical** Works.

47 **Goldsmith's (Oliver) Poems,** Dramas, and the Vicar of Wakefield.

48 **The Koran—The Alkoran** of Mohammed. Translated into English from the Original Arabic, with Explanatory Notes and a Preliminary Discourse. By GEO. SALE.

49 **Oxenford's French Songs.** Including COSTELLO'S Lays of the Troubadours. Finely Illustrated.

50 **Gil Blas (The Adventures** of). By LE SAGE. Translated from the French, with Notes and Illustrations.

51 **The Talmud** (Selections from). Translated from the Original by H. POLANO.

52 **Virgil (Dryden's)** (The Works of). With Index and Life of Virgil.

53 **Bunyan's Holy War.** A Large Type Edition. Illustrated.

54 **Dodd's Beauties of Shaks-** peare.

55 **The Romance of London.** Historic Sketches, Remarkable Duels, Notorious Highwaymen, Rogueries, Crimes and Punishments, &c. By JOHN TIMBS, F.S.A.

THE CHANDOS CLASSICS—*continued.*

THE CHANDOS CLASSICS—continued.

97† **D'Israeli's (Isaac) Calamities and Quarrels of Authors.**

98† **D'Israeli's (Isaac) Amenities of Literature.** • *

99† Ditto • •

(These New Editions were Edited by his Son, the late EARL OF BEACONSFIELD, K.G., and a Memoir and valuable Notes added.)

100 **Æsop's Fables.** Translated by CROXALL and L'ESTRANGE. With applications, &c., by the Rev. G. F. TOWNSEND, and Illustrated with 110 Choice Wood Engravings.

101 to 106 **Hume's History of England.** Six Vols. From the Invasion of Julius Cæsar to the Abdication of James II. By DAVID HUME, Esq. A New Edition, with the Author's last corrections and improvements, and a short account of the Author's life.

107 **Hawthorne's Tanglewood Tales.**

108 **Southey's Life of Nelson.**

109 **Lord Bacon's Essays.** Including his Moral and Historical Works, Advancement of Learning, New Atlantis, &c., with Memoir, Notes, and Glossary.

110† **Plutarch's Lives. (Grecian.)** Agesilaus to Theseus. *

111† **Plutarch's Lives. (Grecian.)** Alexander to Timoleon. * *

112† **Plutarch's Lives. (Roman.)** C. Gracchus to T. Q. Flaminius. * * *

113† **Plutarch's Lives. (Roman.)** Cato the Younger to Pompey the Great. * * * * (Langhorne's Translation.)

114 **Baron Munchausen** (The Travels and Surprising Adventures of). Illustrated with Thirty-seven Curious Engravings from the Baron's own designs, and Five Woodcuts by GEORGE CRUIKSHANK.

115 **Hawthorne's Mosses from an Old Manse.**

116 **Willmott's Poets of the Nineteenth Century.** Selected and Edited by the Rev. ROBERT ARIS WILLMOTT. Illustrated by 130 Original Engravings.

117 to 119 **The Rise of the Dutch Republic.** Three Vols. By JOHN LOTHROP MOTLEY.

120 **Goethe's Faust.** Translated by BAYARD TAYLOR.

121 **Pilpay's Fables.** Illust.

122 **The Shah Nameh** (of the Persian Poet, Firdausi). Translated by ATKINSON.

123 **The Percy Anecdotes.** •

124 Ditto • •

125 Ditto • • •

126 Ditto • • • •

(A Verbatim Reprint of the Original Edition, with a Preface by JOHN TIMBS, F.S.A.)

127 **Schiller's Poems and Ballads.** Translated by Lord LYTTON.

128 **The Spectator.** Selected and Edited by A. C. EWALD.

129 **The Tatler.** Selected and Edited by A. C. EWALD.

130 **Poe (Edgar Allan.)** The Poems and Essays on Poetry, &c., and his Narrative of Arthur Gordon Pym. Edited by JOHN H. INGRAM.

131 **The Ingoldsby Legends.** By the Rev. R. H. BARHAM. Illustrated by CRUIKSHANK and LEECH.

132 **Horace (The Works of).** The Odes, Epodes, Satires, and Epistles translated by the most eminent English Scholars and Poets.

Press Notices.

The TIMES says:—"Thanks to Messrs. Warne and Co.'s 'CHANDOS CLASSICS,' it is in the power of anyone to become possessed of a very respectable library — respectable both in quantity and quality—for a sum of money that some years ago would hardly have sufficed to place one complete edition of a good writer on the bookshelf."

The WHITEHALL REVIEW says:—"A very high meed of praise is due to the handsome volumes with which Messrs. Warne have enriched that most admirable series, 'THE CHANDOS CLASSICS.' 'THE CHANDOS CLASSICS' began many years ago, when the idea of cheap and good books was stranger to the public mind than it is now, and it has since proved a strong and steadily increasing factor in the solution of the problem of popular education."

Price 2s. each.

THE STANLEY LIBRARY.

The Stanley Library Volumes are specially suitable for boys. They consist of healthy, stirring stories of school life, and adventure by land and sea.

In crown 8vo, cloth gilt, extra.

THE KING'S BELL TOWER: A Romance of the Olden Time. By R. ANDRÉ. With Original Illustrations by A. W. COOPER.

"Mr. André's romance is marked by much vigour and by great beauty of style." — *County Gentleman.*

THE TREASURE FINDER: A Story of a Lost Galleon. By W. J. GORDON. With Original Illustrations by W. S. STACEY.

"This is a well-written story, full of incident, never flagging, and thoroughly wholesome. The illustrations are vigorous and well drawn."—*The People.*

JACK LOCKE: A Tale of the War and the Wave. By Dr. GORDON STABLES. With Original Illustrations by F. A. FRASER.

"This is a capital tale for boys, written in Dr. Gordon Stables' well-known high-spirited and dashing manner."—*County Gentleman.*

ERNEST FAIRFIELD; or, Two Terms at St. Andrew's. By the Rev. A. N. MALAN, M.A. With Original Illustrations by F. A. FRASER.

"This is an excellent story agreeably told. The school scenes are very life-like, and the moral of Fairfield's experiences is all that need be desired."—*Spectator.*

THE INCIDENT AND ADVENTURE LIBRARY.

In crown 8vo, cloth gilt extra.

EVENINGS AT HOME. By Dr. AIKIN and Mrs. BARBAULD. With Original Illustrations.

SANDFORD AND MERTON (THE HISTORY OF). By THOMAS DAY. With Original Illustrations.

ROBINSON CRUSOE: His Life and Adventures. By DANIEL DEFOE. With numerous Original Illustrations by ERNEST GRISET and an Introduction and Glossary.

THE SWISS FAMILY ROBINSON; or, Adventures in a Desolate Island. With numerous Original Illustrations.

WILLIS THE PILOT; or, The After Adventures of the Swiss Family Robinson. With Original Illustrations.

THE SILVER CUP; or, True Heroism. A Book for Boys. With Original Illustrations.

ST. GEORGE'S KEY. By the Rev. W. E. COGHLAN, B.A. With Original Illustrations.

"A tale of adventure in the West Indies."

WASHED ASHORE; or, The Tower of Stormount Bay. By W. H. G. KINGSTON. With Original Illustrations.

"A healthy and stirring tale of sea life for boys."

Price 7s. 6d. each.

THE CHANDOS POETS.

The Volumes in this Series are all choicely printed, with red-line border, and ably Edited, and Illustrated with Original Wood Engravings and Steel Portraits.

In imperial 16mo, cloth gilt, gilt edges;
ALSO KEPT
In Turkey morocco, extra.

The Legendary Ballads of England and Scotland.

Eliza Cook's Poetical Works. Complete Edition.

Cowper's (William) Poetical Works. With Memoir, Notes, &c.

Campbell's (Thomas) Poetical Works. With Memoir, Explanatory Notes, &c.

Coleridge's (Samuel Taylor) Poetical Works. With Life, Notes, &c.

Montgomery's (James) Poetical Works. With Memoir and Notes.

Pope's (Alexander) Poetical Works. With Memoir, Explanatory Notes, &c.

Herbert's (George) Works in Prose and Verse. With Memoir, Notes, &c.

THE ALBION POETS.

This Series of the Works of our most widely-read Poets is the most complete and undoubtedly the most popular Edition issued.

The Volumes are all uniform in size, they are clearly printed from large type on excellent paper, and strongly and tastily bound in the following styles:

Price 5s. each.
In cloth, gilt top, leather label, gilt lettered, hand-trimmed to give large margin, with a Steel Portrait;

Price 3s. 6d. each.
In imperial 16mo, cloth gilt (neat style).
ALSO KEPT
In French morocco, red under gold edges, in box.
In full calf, red under gold edges, in box.

Shakspeare's Complete Works. 1,152 pages.

Lord Byron's Poetical Works. With Explanatory Notes. 736 pages.

H. W. Longfellow's Poetical Works. 638 pages.

Sir Walter Scott's Poetical Works. With Notes, &c. 766 pages.

Milton's Poetical Works. With Explanatory Notes, &c.

Gems of National Poetry. 1,000 Selections.

Wordsworth's Poetical Works. With Memoir, Appendix, &c. 672 pages.

Robert Burns' Poetical Works. With Explanatory Notes. 640 pages.

Shelley's Poetical Works. With Life and Notes. 640 pages.

The Ingoldsby Legends. By R. H. BARHAM. With Life and Illusts.

The Vision of Dante: Hell, Purgatory and Paradise. With Life Notes, &c. CARY'S Translation.

Price 3s. 6d. each.

THE LANSDOWNE POETS.

ENTIRELY NEW EDITIONS, WELL PRINTED, WITH OXFORD
RED-LINE BORDER

Carefully Edited, with Original Notes, Steel Portraits and full-page Illustrations.

In crown 8vo, cloth, extra gilt, and gilt edges ;
ALSO KEPT
In French morocco limp, and padded morocco extra.

Shakspeare's (William) Complete Works. With Life and Glossary.

Longfellow's (Henry W.) Poetical Works. Including Recent Poems.

Byron's (Lord) Poetical Works. Complete.

Eliza Cook's Poetical Works.

Scott's (Sir Walter) Poetical Works.

Moore's (Thomas) Poetical Works. With Life and Memoir.

Cowper's (William) Poetical Works. With Memoir.

Milton's (John) Poetical Works

Wordsworth's (William) Poetical Works. With Life, &c.

Mrs. Hemans' Poetical Works.

Keble's (Rev. John) The Christian Year. Thoughts in Verse for Sundays and Holy Days throughout the Year.

Burns' (Robert) Poetical Works. With Glossary and Memoir.

Hood's (Thos.) Poetical Works. Complete Edition, with Memoir.

Coleridge's (Samuel Taylor) Poetical Works.

Shelley's (Percy Bysshe) Poetical Works.

Pope's (Alexander) Poetical Works. With Memoir.

Goldsmith's (Oliver) Poems and Plays. With "The Vicar of Wakefield."

Montgomery's (James) Poetical Works.

Heber's (Bishop) Poetical Works. Fully Illustrated.

Herbert's (George) Works in Prose and Verse.

Dodd's Beauties of Shakspeare.

Gray, Beattie and Collins : The Poetical Works of.

Percy's Reliques of Ancient Poetry. Consisting of Old Heroic Ballads, Songs, &c. Edited by E. WALFORD, M.A.

Dante (The Vision of.) Hell, Purgatory and Paradise. Translated by Rev. H. F. CARY, A.M.

Goethe's Faust. Translated by BAYARD TAYLOR.

Schiller's Poems and Ballads. By Sir EDWARD BULWER LYTTON, Bart.

Poe's (Edgar Allan) Poetical Works and Essays on Poetry. With his Narrative of ARTHUR GORDON PYM.

Also uniform, without Red-line Border.

The Poets of the Nineteenth Century. Selected by the Rev. ROBERT ARIS WILMOTT. With 130 Choice Illustrations.

Campbell's (Thomas) Poetical Works. With Memoir, &c.

Keats' (John) Poetical Works. With Memoir, &c.

Spenser's (Edmund) Poetical Works. With Glossary, &c.

Songs, Sacred and Devotional.

Golden Leaves from the American Poets.

The Legendary Ballads of England and Scotland.

Johnson's Lives of the Poets. With a Sketch of the Author's Life by Sir WALTER SCOTT.

Laurel and Lyre.

Price 3s. 6d. per Volume.

THE CAVENDISH LIBRARY.

A Series of Standard Works in English Literature, printed on super-fine paper and uniformly bound in neat Library style.

In large crown 8vo, cloth gilt, uncut edges.

HALF-HOURS WITH THE BEST AUTHORS. Edited by CHARLES KNIGHT. In Four Volumes, with Steel Frontispieces.

Each Volume contains Extracts from our Great Standard Authors, including MACAULAY, THACKERAY, DICKENS, CHARLES KINGSLEY, DE QUINCEY, MILTON, GEORGE ELIOT, and others.

HALF-HOURS OF ENGLISH HISTORY. In Four Volumes, with Steel Frontispieces.

Edited by CHARLES KNIGHT.

Vol. I. From the Roman Period to the Death of Henry III.

Vol. II. From Edward I. to the Death of Elizabeth.

Edited by L. VALENTINE.

Vol. III. From James I. to William and Mary.

Vol. IV. From Anne to Victoria.

THE RISE OF THE DUTCH REPUBLIC. By JOHN LOTHROP MOTLEY. Complete Edition. In Three Volumes, with Notes, Index, &c.

HISTORY OF THE WAR IN THE PENINSULA, and in the South of France from the Year 1807 to the Year 1814. By Major-General W. F. P. NAPIER, C.B. In Six Volumes, with Notes, Steel Portrait, and 55 Maps and Plans.

HALF-HOURS WITH THE BEST AMERICAN AUTHORS. Selected and Edited by CHARLES MORRIS. In Four Volumes, with Steel Frontispieces.

Each Volume contains Extracts from the following Authors; MARK TWAIN, OLIVER WENDELL HOLMES, WASHINGTON IRVING, J. R. LOWELL, LONGFELLOW, POE, PRESCOTT and others.

EVELYN'S DIARY AND CORRESPONDENCE. Edited by WILLIAM BRAY, Esq. With Steel Frontispiece and full Index.

LEIGH HUNT, as Poet and Essayist. Being the Choicest Passages from his Works, Selected and Edited, with a Biographical Introduction, by CHARLES KENT. With Steel Portrait.

"This memoir is both generous and discreet. Mr. Kent's feeling for the man is as clear as his admiration for the writer. He has, in short, written precisely as a friend should write, but as friends too rarely do write in these long-winded days; not a word too much, and yet omitting nothing which could show us the man at his best—a well-drawn, well-composed, genuine little piece of portraiture."—*World.*

THE LIFE OF WESLEY, and the Rise and Progress of Methodism. By ROBERT SOUTHEY. Edited by the Rev. J. A. ATKINSON, M.A., D.C.L. With Steel Portrait.

This excellent and valuable biography has well fulfilled the expectations of its author, and the present Editor has done his work with care and skill.

In this edition almost every work on the subject published since "Southey's Life" was issued has been read and consulted in its preparation, and New Notes added.

PEPYS' DIARY AND CORRESPONDENCE. Edited by Lord BRAYBROOKE. With Steel Frontispiece, Portrait and full Index.

www.ingramcontent.com/pod-product-compliance
Lightning Source LLC
Chambersburg PA
CBHW030600040726
47497CB00008B/2807